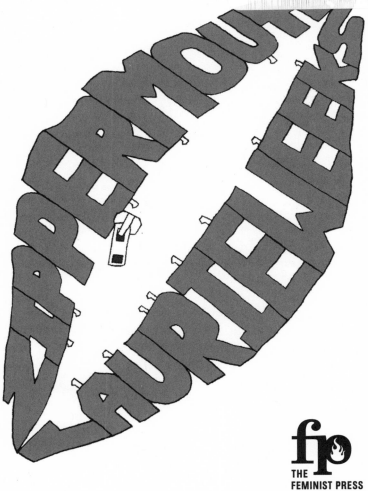

ZIPPERMOUTH

LAURIE WEEKS

fp
THE
FEMINIST PRESS
AT THE CITY UNIVERSITY
OF NEW YORK
NEW YORK CITY

Published in 2011 by the Feminist Press
at the City University of New York
The Graduate Center
365 Fifth Avenue, Suite 5406
New York, NY 10016

feministpress.org

First printing May 2011

Cover design by Herb Thornby, herbthornby.com
Text design by Drew Stevens

Library of Congress Cataloging-in-Publication Data

Weeks, Laurie.
Zipper mouth / by Laurie Weeks.
    p. cm.
ISBN 978-1-55861-748-3
I. Title.
PS3623.E4224Z57 2011
813'.6—dc22
                    2011014853

for

Lea Baechler
1952–2004

&

Danny Tulip
1964–2004

As reason returned to me, memory came with it, and I saw that even on the worst days, when I thought I was utterly and completely miserable, I was nevertheless, and nearly all the time, extremely happy. That gave me something to think about.

—Maurice Blanchot,
The Madness of the Day

Movie: *Of Human Bondage* (1934) A clubfooted medical student is infatuated with a woman.

—*NY Post* TV listing

I decided I was in love with this girl and I couldn't eat, couldn't sleep. I smoked cigarettes and lay on the bed. I wanted her to drop by in the afternoon for a nap. It didn't seem likely but this was part of the pleasure, like the agony of fixating on a dead movie star the way I'd become obsessed at age fifteen with the long-decomposed actress Vivien Leigh, a.k.a. Scarlett O'Hara, and her later, more bummed-out incarnation, Blanche DuBois. Instead of rock stars, I had pictures of Vivien all over my room, glossy publicity shots and film stills I'd ordered or simply received in the mail, gifts from sad obsessives who advertised, as I did, in the back pages of *Nostalgia, Illustrated*, a creepy classic-movie magazine for shut-ins and losers that I'd stumbled across on the racks at Consumer's Supermarket while leafing through *Seventeen* and holding my breath against the stench from the sugar beet factory squatting evilly down the road. At night I lay awake in sadness, grieving that Vivien had died alone, coughing herself to death consumptively long before I was old enough to intervene.

ZIPPER MOUTH

"She was a great actress," I said morosely to my friends, trying to visualize her having sex with Laurence Olivier, not so easy, really, to wrap your mind around. Part of her allure was the fact that she spelled "Vivien" with an *e,* not an *a,* the *e* more refined and seductive, the *a* somehow thudding and crude, witness the barbarian Vivian Vance.

In one of the photos tacked up inside my teenage closet, Vivien leans into the lens and smiles, glamorous in the low-cut red velvet robe she wore in *Gone With the Wind* when Rhett takes her upstairs and rapes her, at which point she blossoms into the fullness of her love. The shot's a medium close-up taken as she relaxes on the set, in her hand a cigarette. She's smoking. Each day after school I'd lock my bedroom door, open the closet, and stand with my peanut butter sandwich, staring into Vivien's green eyes as if my gaze, held long enough, could jump-start the pulse in her throat, compel the hand with that cigarette off the page and up to my lips to offer me a drag, her body following to step gracefully into my room, suspended tobacco smoke drawn back into the chamber of her mouth as she starts to breathe again for real. Jesus, I couldn't imagine: Mom vacuuming the same spot suspiciously outside my door while inside there's this movie star *thing* looking into your eyes. Oh my god you just want to be the smoke pulled between her lips. What happens when you get inside a person anyway, up that close, inside their mouth? Nothing, I guess. It's like a photograph blown up. They just dissolve into a haze of black and white dots until all you have is molecules and air, nothing there.

That day on the sidewalk you lifted your arm above your head. There in the hollow the wispy dark hairlets, I couldn't breathe. I lit a cigarette, walked inside a building. Dreamily I got through my task, propelled by shots of adrenaline at the thought of your name. The job was easy, I didn't care. I drifted home, not minding the sidewalk, the wreckage percolating around me. Your name is Jane. I floated through my door, lit a cigarette, my nerves were black. I thought I might buy some drugs and call you up.

"I'm a Scorpio," Vivien explained to a reporter, "and we Scorpios are like that: we eat ourselves up and burn ourselves out." At fifteen, I lumbered numbly through various hallways—from my bedroom to the kitchen, from the snack bar to math. In geometry I sat there flunking and stared with loathing at my forearm: it looked so meaty. Whenever the guy next to me glanced over, I hid it in my lap. I had long, thin limbs but in my mind I was a sausage, the wrapping stretched tight to the point of bursting with a putrid, ground-up meat. I pictured the finespun Vivien huddled in the corner of a darkened hotel room in Rome, abandoned by Olivier, career on the rocks, cold flames rolling off her, burning alive in the firestorm of her manic depression. I watched the scorpion stinger on her tail, stuck in her own throat and convulsively pushing poison into her neck. Something that doesn't hurt one part of your body can leak from its sac and paralyze another.

Dear Rolf:

I wanted to say something about Vivien that your letter reminded me of. You know, her death was such a devastating thing for everyone concerned that it had a strong effect on me. As a result, I've been trying to overcome my affinity for Vivien by ignoring everything about her. Of course this is ridiculous, because I love acting, and she is the best actress I've ever seen, yet undeniably wild under the surface. In a more concrete area, you mentioned that you felt her hair was much too severe. However, just before you wrote that, I was thinking how much I liked her hair as she got older, because she wasn't teasing it. But then I got to thinking, and the more I thought, the sadder I got. Thinking of Vivien generally makes me unhappy. Yesterday an article mentioned she was cremated. Everything slammed to a halt. I knew it now. She was dead, and she was gone. She didn't exist, there was nothing left, it was exactly like seeing a living person vanish into thin air. I had the eerie feeling I was looking into London and seeing only sky. Well, it is sad but of course it is the best possible thing. One has to come to terms

sometime, it's strange and difficult to know someone through descriptions and words. Plus I think
it's very trite for the Vivien Leigh Society to sign
their letters Sincere-Leigh.

I looked down at the copy before me, which I was supposed to proofread. Jesus Christ, I couldn't focus.
I sat back in my chair, fiddling with the pen, my eyes
moving around the room of their own accord, wandering orbs of a vegetative patient. Thin strip of blue visible above the building opposite. My gaze dragged my
body across the room and out the large sealed window,
over the desk littered with drafts, book blurbs to check,
sticks of gum I chewed obsessively for fear of offending
my co-workers, whom I loathed, the various staplers
and paper clips, over the crowded desktop past the
trash can filled with signifiers of my incompetence—
incorrect printouts, Coke cans to nurse my hangover,
plastic trays from the cafeteria since I couldn't get it
together to bring my lunch—my gaze pulled me across
the stained beige carpet and through the window, then
it let me go. An open space opened in my chest. This
was love, a ledge. I stepped off to plunge through the
icy blue. Jane, the falling sensation. So cold my burning
skin. Falling past windows I am many people, each with

a body temperature unique to them. Some are feverish and some hypothermic, trailing flames or bits of ice. Some have diabetes, some have twenty-twenty vision, many are blind. A few of my personalities can enjoy the occasional Snickers bar and then not think about chocolate or indeed any candy at all for days. Similarly, some of my selves are tormented by nicotine addiction while others can enjoy a cigarette or two and never have one again. Some of my personalities have had three or four amputations. Others successfully manage a variety of apartment complexes. Some languish in comas, a few go fly-fishing with their fathers, others sneer at cheap sentiment. One of my personalities was a concubine for a homicidal dictator and was never able to get adequate medical treatment for her resulting syphilis.

Dear So-and-So, I'm sorry I didn't call you back but I've been really really sick.

I glanced again at the pack of lies awaiting my scrutiny on the desk. Fuck. I pushed my chair away from the desk and began leafing through a book nabbed from the Free Shelves in the hall. "Do you have those pages for me yet?" I looked up. In the doorway stood Sue, chief editor or something. "What are you doing?" she said, glancing at the book. Its title, *Living Without a Goal*, appealed to me, though when opened it turned out the dust jacket had erroneously been placed over galleys of a book about the bombing of Dresden. "This isn't the time to be doing your personal business," said Sue. "I was just doing a little fact-checking," I replied, tapping the book confidently before tossing it aside and pretending to jot some pertinent info on a lime sticky. Sue lingered a moment, her eyes coating me with distaste. Busily I finished scribbling *I Am a Total Cunt: Sue's Story* on the sticky. "I need those pages now," she said finally, turning away. "Have them for you in a second," I sang amiably as she moved off. Don't look at me. What's alien about yourself is intolerable; you expel it onto me. Your displaced selves clutch at my hair, miniature psychotic children twirling from the maypole of my body spinning in your eyes.

Once I was twelve, riding my bike at night on a country road in pitch blackness. I passed by the only street lamp for miles. My shadow shot across the road onto a wall of hedges. On the leaves a perfect outline: bike wheels, pedals, legs bending and going around, torso leaning over the handlebars, crooked arms, round ball for my head. Of course there will come a time when I won't have a body and hence no shadow.

I crumpled the sticky then on second thought smoothed it out and taped it to the cover of the Dresden book beneath the *Living Without a Goal* dust jacket. I dropped my head to the desk, my mind wandered back to the night before. Thinking of your lips, a kiss that makes your heart lurch. I didn't kiss you last night. I lay awake by myself in a drunken trance of imagined kisses.

Valerie, another editorial overlord, patrolled past my door in a fuchsia suit patterned with enormous flowers, the mutant blossoms shouting for release from the cheap fabric. Her brown and placid hair lay unassailable in its barrette. Swampily, I observed her from my den, mesmerized by the strange and gaseous colors of the garment even as my fingers pounded industriously at the keyboard. *Jane*, I typed again and again, trying to imagine how it would feel to be named Jane. *Jane.*

During the lengthy delirium of my romance with Vivien Leigh, *a long illness which took place entirely within the mysteries of my soul,* as Mallarmé put it, I was possessed by a monomaniacal lust for tidbits about Vivien, accounts of her ecstasies and torment, her favorite songs, hints of the savage intelligence and raging hungers I envisioned surging beneath her exquisitely controlled demeanor. At the mall I haunted the theater and film shelves of Waldenbooks in an altered state while stoners in the dark arcade across the hall played Asteroids and foosball, at which my friend Stacey and I regularly kicked their contemptuous weaselly asses in pizza parlors all over town. "Ugly bitches," they'd mutter, shoving quarter after quarter into the coin slot. In the bookstore, deaf to the neural disruption of electronic

sirens and beeps and the hard slap of plastic disks rico-
cheting across the air hockey table table, I scanned
indexes until Vivien's name appeared, its letters curare-
tipped arrows causing my hyperventilating sensorium
to seize as I spastically mangled my way through the
book to the magic page. When movie books arrived in
the mail I tore through the envelopes as though ripping
off her clothes. Brief exposures surfaced. Vivien folding
her panty hose each day in the shape of a cross, a life-
long eccentricity. Vivien eating lunch each day facing
a Modigliani or a Dufy. Vivien *adoring* any lunch eaten
while facing a Modigliani or a Dufy. Favorite hobby,
Miss Leigh? *Serendipity.* Vivien en route to the sanitarium, stepping from a small 1950s plane to collapse
into the arms of Danny Kaye on the tarmac, an embrace
that made the hair on my forearms stand up as though
I were about to be struck by lightning.

Lorraine, one of my fanatical correspondents, fed
her void within by viewing Vivien vehicles like *Water-
loo Bridge* on all-night TV in the magical world of NYC,
whereas our four local stations signed off at midnight.
I considered writing PBS to ask for some Leigh films
but it seemed futile—I imagined my request buried
beneath thousands of postcards delivered each day to
the station, an avalanche fired off by my town's miniscule population, specific titles itemized during chain-
smoking breaks at the beet factory or interludes atop

idling tractors, some guy throwing the engine into neutral mid-plow for no reason. Spaced out in the glowing neutrino flow ejected by the sun, your endocrine system in thrall to the silky drift of Aldicarb and Nitrofen motes shed by crop dusters skimming the fields. *Dear PBS, Could you please show that one movie where James Dean and Natalie Wood fall in love beneath stars in a planetarium, or else another very sad one where Natalie Wood and Warren Beatty have the most magical heartbreaking love.*

Who was I? Answer: Nobody. Management would trash my plea without even bothering to read it. On the other hand, was it not the moral of all Katharine Hepburn vehicles and Hollywood anecdotes in general that really only eccentricity and saucy effrontery distinguished you from the mindless herd and made people respect you enough to do your bidding? In fifth period Social Studies, while my debate partner arranged M&M's in fanciful patterns on her thigh under the desk and ate them one by one according to a complicated algorithm, my mind wandered out the window and strode into the office of the PBS boss, Spencer Tracy, to demand with wit and spunk that he show some guts for once in his life and act like a man by screening something smart, rather than playing lackey to the mouth-breathing tastes of the Sheep. Classy flicks, things like, oh, say, films starring Vivien Leigh, for example.

Leaning over the desk to torch his cigar with my chrome pistol-shaped lighter, I pin him against the leather chair with my flashing eyes. "And get a grip on the Three Motherfucking Stooges, ok? Show something else." I snap the lighter shut. "Like maybe some self-respect." Whirling, I'd stride from the room, leaving Spencer awestruck, stricken, cut to the bone by truth and desperately in love. That night, PBS breaks into *An American Family* with an urgent bulletin announcing a very special tribute to legendary British actress Vivien Leigh and her groundbreaking films, a marathon extravaganza running the gamut from fluff like *Look Up and Laugh* to sexy total bummers like Tennessee Williams's *The Roman Spring of Mrs. Stone*, featuring Warren Beatty as the Italian gigolo who crushes Vivien's aging heart like a freshly drained can of Coors in the fist of a frat boy. The promo ends, the phone rings.

It's Spencer. "You're a spoiled brat and somebody oughta teach you a lesson," he growls. "Oh yeah?" I say. "Yeah," he says. "Well, in that case, Professor," I purr, "I'll be at Tiny's in the mall next to the Chuckwagon Buffet. 7:30. Maybe you'd like to drop by and show me your syllabus. I could use a laugh. Oh, PS—I do my best studying over a Stinger or three. And I never pay." Click.

My genius strategy was to type Vivien's name hundreds of times on a single sheet of paper. Surely this would catch the eye of those PBS philistines. *Vivien*

Leigh Vivien Leigh Vivien Leigh, row after row of *Vivien Leigh*, I typed, like Jack Nicholson tapping out "All work and no play makes Jack a dull boy" in *The Shining*. Even in my delusional state, however, I registered the vibe of weirdness rising from the onionskin paper when I pulled it from the typewriter, and stowed the sheet away in a folder of creative writing fantasies sodden with melancholy, starring Miss Vivien Leigh.

Valerie strolled by again. I'd typed *Jane* so many times that the word no longer computed, producing a faint disorientation hinting at out-of-body experiences that I sort of enjoyed. Valerie's legs rubbed against one another in their pumps and I could hear her skirt grating against the frayed mesh of her tortured nylons. The carpeted office floor surged beneath me. I rose and grabbed my bag. I should take the edge off a little, maybe—it would help my productivity.

"Dude," I said compulsively, passing another temp in the hall as I raced to the bathroom. He looked away. I was quite possibly the most ludicrous person on earth, was I not? In the bathroom I swallowed a fistful of Tylenol #4s and adjusted the complicated winch-and-pulley system of my bra so that it might hoist my breasts into a more salable elevation. My aura was piss yellow, I felt smothered in my own vapor, an inert gas of vinegary poisons. I rinsed my forehead and leaned against the sink. I feel hot, I am sweating, my skin hangs sallow and flaccid in the fluorescent downpour from the buzzing light tubes. My shirt was simple but ugly. I sat down on a toilet and closed the stall. I opened a wee envelope and tapped a bit of the powder I'd scored from some shady street entity onto the back of my hand, onto the bridge of skin between thumb and forefinger which I enjoyed referring to as "the web of snorting." I did a bump of the powder, tapped out some more, did another. I sometimes felt I had to go into the bathroom to escape the bathroom, deeper and deeper into the bathroom to sniff up the drugs that would catapult me beyond the restroom-like confines of my mind, the petty yet viselike humiliation of runny noses and pee and other things I can't bring myself to mention, the shameful effluent of having been born.

In seventh grade, walking from the football field to Wheeler's Drive-In for some french fries after school, I'm spaced out as usual, contemplating the issues of the day such as do I have enough change for a Coke, when a girl even less popular than I am sneers and says to me, "Why don't you stand up straight?" Mortified, I have no idea what she's talking about. I was just walking along the strip. Here is the body, which, being inside itself, knows no size or shape. "Take a picture, it'll last longer." What? But I didn't even *see* you! Not a body so much as an amorphous state. People tell you to walk upright, to sit up straight: you hadn't known you were slanting forward. You're just a head, an awareness, your body might as well be a vat in which your consciousness floats and expands like a kombucha mushroom.

Will these drugs give me necrotizing fasciitis, the deadly flesh-eating bacteria, I wonder? I recalled the story of two girls who had died after shooting heroin smuggled across the border in cadavers. A pack of women clacked in on high heels, discussing the usual topic, lunch. There seemed also to be some concern about the Planet. Over the sound of faucets running, paper towels pulled from the dispenser, purses clicking shut, I overheard one girl remark in exasperation, "Oh c'mon. Does anyone really care if the manatees go extinct?" I stood up in the stall and shoved the envelope into my purse, no, not my purse, my bag. *I hate that word, "purse,"* I reflected. *Why is that, I wonder?* Abruptly, well-being surged through me, proving the drug to be either speed or heavily cut coke, as opposed to the baking soda I'd feared. Actually, I realized, this job was fantastic. It's not like I was stuck in a meatpacking plant or at Eton Publishing, a morgue-like porn factory where I sat in a roomful of temps, all of us rigid with embarrassment, pretending we weren't typesetting hardcore copy consisting primarily of phrases like "pulsating manstick" and "tight wet" whatever, the assignment in my case being *Family Touch*, a magazine for truckers which exposed the national epidemic of sixteen-year-old suburban whores whose mission it is to seduce their hapless stepdads into after-school sex while Mom's in the hospital giving birth to yet another nymphomaniac. Here, on the other hand, I had my own office and the supplies necessary to conduct my private affairs. Really, not only were things fine, they were excellent. Putting on what I imagined to be the face of competence and goodwill, I emerged from the ladies' room to find myself swept up in a river of VPs, copy editors, receptionists, and techs stam ed-ing toward the employee cafeteria. Happily I sat down before my computer, bombarded with insights, fingers racing to compose an amusing and heartfelt email to a beloved friend. Sue bustled past. "Almost done, Sue," I called out sunnily as she disappeared around a corner.

One of the first times we hung out Jane said to me, "So what have you been doing?" The answer was, "Dope." Or "Staying hungover in bed, waiting for a check, contemplating suicide and TV." But I said, "Oh, you know. Hiding, mostly, avoiding phone calls from annoying people who want to be my friend." Jane laughed. She goes, "I guess I'm one of those annoy-ing people who wants to be your friend." Insect wings fluttered in my chest. No. She was straight. We were walking down a sidewalk. I said, "Let's go in this store and buy enormous alcoholic-size cans of beer." "Good thinking," Jane said. "And cigarettes." Technically speaking, of course, I wasn't supposed to drink but I did get drunk with Jane. It seemed like nothing bad could happen if you were drinking with Jane, she made it feel so elegant, just what you should be doing. She drank martinis and Manhattans in the classic cocktail glass. Going out with her felt like being in a movie made back when drinking and smoking were just the ticket.

Random surge of loneliness, a rush almost like a craving for a cigarette. You're in it, it's a suction, a whirl-pool, then it's over, you're on to the next thing, toast or whatever. Jane, probably sleeping. Rainy 4 a.m., a pack of drug dealers on the corner. The gleaming streets, desire rushes up from the wet black pavement to pull me down. I could go downstairs, say to the guy, "What do you sell?" Last night I simply wanted to kiss Jane goodbye on the cheek, but she hooked me with her gaze and turned her lips toward me. I couldn't believe it, my intentions were toward her cheek or at most the corner of her lips but suddenly there I was, falling headlong into her mouth. Her lips came toward mine and she held me with her eyes. Then suddenly her mouth was gone and my lips grazed her cheek. "Okay," she smiled, picking up her drink. "Very, very fine. Get home safe."

In my dream I took an elevator up to the wrong apartment. It shot me into the center of my childhood living room with the love seats and Venus flytrap. I'd pushed the button for Jane's floor. Now the elevator was a golden field of buttercups, green irises, and nasturtiums. A silver dog named Lily twirled and nosed around. What can this mean: Jane's eyes are green. There were sinister characters, of course, lurking outside the apartment door. Also, I think, a parade. I sat down in my mother's love seat. Shadows from the clouds swept across the flowers and birds wheeled and currents of air undulated through the grass, phantom snakes. Then the air went still, the birds vanished, and something began moving across the sky from the horizon, a sheet of glass gliding overhead with a machinic hum until I was sealed beneath it in the field, in a paperweight or crystal ball. "Don't worry," Jane said, materializing beside me on the love seat. She leaned over, lifted my hair, and kissed my neck. I was so glad to see her. Her breath was warm and it tickled. "I have some airplane glue in my purse," she whispered, biting my lower lip.

From the dream I came thwacking into consciousness against my pillow like a bullet lodging in a lung. Noxious fumes roiled into the room from supply trucks thundering outside. The TV bled soundlessly across my sheets from atop the dresser. Elasticized mouths uncoiled onscreen and teeth issued from the rubbery flesh. The TV was always on. Usually I liked the blue light, the colors leaking across me, the long hair of girls onscreen. I like girls with dark hair. Now that I'm in love with you I feel like that stinky girl at the edge of the playground. I thought, Does Jane ever wake from a little fever dream of me tangling fingers in her hair to pull her head back? Has it ever happened even once that she pushed the sheets off, bitter they weren't me, and moved around her kitchen making coffee in a haze, unhinged by love, brushing her teeth with Neosporin?

In third grade, at my desk listening to Mrs. Woodward read *Charlotte's Web*, my daydreaming mind was like an insect on codeine at the circus: tiny, weightless, winged and acrobatic, flipping opiated through the air from a trapeze to alight on the tightrope, scalps and shirtsleeves from the crowd below swarming in through my multifaceted eyes a cloud of multicolored cells. I'd sit for a minute on the tightrope then lift off to drift drugged above the cheering voices on air currents from their breath. Just for fun I might tumble down and down to the landing pad of an elephant, nestling into the stalks of fur for a ride around the ring that set me humming a cheerful tune. I might sneak up to his forehead and execute some mischievous somersaults between his oceanic eyes, those deceptively placid pools over which a hidden trapdoor could slide shut and crush you in an instant. Not me. When I'd had my fun I'd use his trunk for a diving board, springing *boing boing* to catch another wave of exhalation from the crowd.

In my floaty delirium I rode the surf of Mrs. Woodward's voice, which I got mixed up with Charlotte the gentle spider, but how could you be in love with a spider? I wanted Mrs. Woodward to visit my mom for tea, so she could see my room and my shelves and how I lived. I wouldn't climb into her lap, of course, but I'd want to. Sadly, my brother would ride his tricycle down the porch steps and crack his head open on the sidewalk. Blood everywhere and a rush to the hospital, trike overturned in the yard. He'd be okay, of course, but for the moment Mrs. Woodward would stay behind with me. She'd say, "Now I think it's time for your nap. You're upset; come and lie down with me." In my room she'd close the door, sit me down on the bed, help untie my shoes. She'd stroke my hair and say, "It's okay, don't be sad." She herself had to be wearing something different from the hideous garments she wore to school; certainly she couldn't have on panty hose or those creepy brown pumps. The word *pumps* made me hate her. For a daring instant I tried to picture her naked, standing in front of the class holding *Charlotte's Web*, but that too filled me with outrage. Also her underwear better not look like my mom's.

Jane and I were walking over by the river. It was late, after 3 a.m., summertime and hot, buckled slabs of concrete gleaming hard and soft in yellow streetlight, the abandoned streets silent except for a hum of air conditioners, vents in the high-rise behind us, millions of cooling systems, fan belts, the breath of the city. I hadn't known her for that long. She said, "Listen, I had a dream about you." I said, "Me? What was I doing?" A rush and whisper of friction produced by car metals sliding past on the highway. "Well," said Jane, lighting a cigarette, "it's kinda weird." She shook the match and dropped it. She said, "I was standing at the top of a mountain and you were down at the bottom on one side and Damon was on the other. I guess I was stuck or something, I couldn't get down. You were way down below me and you were being really nice. Damon couldn't talk. I go, 'I can't come down, I'm scared.' And you go, really sweet, 'Come on, Jane. It's okay. If you just relax, it's easy.' I couldn't decide whether to come down on your side or Damon's." Saying this, Jane laughed. I cast my eyes sideways. Her long thin arm in the sleeveless dress brushed against mine; dark hair curled against her neck. Her pocketbook dangled from her shoulder, slipped back and forth against her hip. "Do you think it's weird I'm telling you this?" she asked, taking a drag off her cigarette and staring straight ahead. It was such a stereotypical Freudian dream that I laughed. Either she was making it up or her unconscious was incredibly dull. I wished my unconscious would send me such easy dreams. Until this very second I'd thought she was a straight girl, everyone said so. She was always following the gigantic Damon around from bar to bar to watch him do his stupid puppet shows, but now, holy shit, a sudden buoyancy surged in my limbs. Jane wasn't stupid, she was flirting. Which meant she wanted me to kiss her, right? Love like liquid Xanax infused my spinal fluid along with a powerful sense of superiority that I'd seen through her clever ruse. A magnetic field flowing from her skin was drugging me. I got reckless. Dark hair, tough profile, sleeveless dress—if she wanted me so bad, she could wait. I reached into her purse for the Marlboros. Stopping, I turned and grabbed her hand, pulled it toward my mouth. I couldn't look her in the eye. While the cherry of her cigarette burned into the unlit tip of my own, I looked over her shoulder, past her white neck, an earlobe, the dyed black hair. Across the Hudson, the huge and sadly festive Colgate clock with its red rim that reminds me of the Ferris wheel in *Under the Volcano*. I suck on the filter, let go of her hand. A breeze running in off the water flirts with her skirt, lifts it.

I'm looking at this picture. I pretend it's you standing next to me but instead it's me and another girl. I pulled it from a drawer. I don't have any photographs of you and me, I'm just superimposing your face on the blurry outline of some friend. We're sort of laughing in the picture, me and this other girl, and my chest blossoms with a pleasurable violence when I imagine you beside me in the photo, as though already we share a narrative of adoration and nostalgia and desperation and need. Would you like me better if you saw this picture? I look okay. My hair looks good. I used to worry that I had a narcissistic personality disorder because I thought about myself so much, but now I just go, *So?* When I think of the way the Existential Prison wraps its feathery rubber straps around your rib cage like an alien life form and begins its long slow compression, I go, *It's a wonder we're all not out of our fucking minds.* Which we are. Of course you have to think about yourself a lot, if only to keep your head from snapping forward on your neck. I get out of bed, make the coffee, call my friends, in spite of this thick Pepto-Bismol of dread circulating in my veins. I keep seeing you and your body whirling away, just out of reach, a sand spout. For what is desire but this dervish drilling into the air a window on the glimmering panorama that flashes into existence the second you think *I'm in love.* As soon as you approach that enchanted space, desire spins it away.

Once I remarked drunkenly to Jane, "You know, it occurred to me recently that my so-called self is naught but a tiny bloodsucking vermin perched atop the back of a giant ox lumbering toward a cliff." "Oh totally," nodded Jane. She blew out a stream of smoke and took a sip of her vodka martini. "And you know what else?" she said. "What?" I said. She pulled the toothpick from her glass. "Whatever way you can find," she said, "to keep your balance on what I like to call the 'Shifting Sands of Reality,' I say to you"—she stabbed the olives in my direction—"that's fine."

"Reflections"
(A Young Girl Looks Back)
by . . . Anonymous (aged eleven years)

There is no escape for me. I hate everyone who ever lived, including other planets. My dad is a monster since fifth grade, before that totally normal and great, I have to stay awake every night planning escape routes for me and my brothers depending on which way he goes first. When I fall asleep, he tries to kill us IN MY DREAM! We run all over the streets like crazy nuts but the houses are empty, no one lives here but us, the neighbors moved away.

True or false: boys hate me. Answer: duh, as proved every day but also today when the popular ones tackled me at lunch and spit on me, even Richie who I thought was my friend. I'm not going to say how I laugh so hard almost every day at MY OWN JOKES that I wet my pants which is freezing wet and have to walk home with my coat around my waist plus sneak my jeans into the washer so Mom doesn't know. My hands were so frozen on

Monday that I couldn't button them back up in the bathroom and got sent to Mr. Durham's office. I had to sneak a valentine onto Mrs. Perko's desk so she wouldn't think I was in love with her.

I would like the world to get all TILTED LIKE GERMAN EXPRESSIONISM just for once!!!!! Which I just saw a book about on Mr. Litsey's desk. Then I would faint. If I was wasting away in a hospital like a deer, very quiet and shy, everyone would feel bad for being blind fuckheads and put me in a foster home. World's greatest dream.

Why you no like winter," the driver states flatly, accelerating through the teeming Saturday night streets, interrogating me about my suspicious relationship to weather, screeching to a halt at an intersection. "Only the winter she comes once a year." I'm stoned on some of Andy's pot I found hidden in a box of X-acto knives at work and filled with a sense of impending doom. "I'm not putting it down," I reply, head snapping back as he guns it when the light turns. "I just don't like being cold." Swerving around a tour bus, the cab hits a pothole and begins a slow-motion glide sideways toward a parked limo. "And your husband?" the driver says. "He no like winter, too?" Oh god, I think as he steers incompetently out of the skid. "My husband," I lie, flinching as the limo flashes by, inches from my window, "likes winter a lot. I just have bad circulation or something." I can sense the cab driver's disapproval of my soft upbringing. "I try to talk myself out of being cold, but it doesn't work. It makes my husband crazy. He's very disciplined." Why am I telling him this? We skid along in silence. "Your husband he no understand you," he muses darkly. "It's okay," I say, "because I'm going to Mexico."

"How is Mexican weather?" he asks, catching my eye in the mirror. "Mexican weather is good," I say. "Mexican weather is great." We decelerate sickeningly then lurch ahead. "It's totally great," I say. The car fishtails through an intersection, nearly flattening a group of club kids in the crosswalk. "I fucking kill you faggots," the driver mutters. He looks back at me again. "Why a man he want to put his parts into another man?"

"I love Mexican weather," I reply. "It's fabulous. I mean, I've never been there but that's why people go. In March or whenever. Which is when I'm going next year. I mean, I don't know much about the weather in this one town where I'm going, but it's Mexico in winter, so I think the weather's always fine. Mexico is known for its winters. Not because they're hard, but rather because they're easy. That's why they have a lot of tourists." Am I having difficulty breathing?

"Your husband is in Mexico?" asks the driver coyly. "This is why you not wearing the ring?" "My husband's waiting for me at home," I say. "Ah." He nods. Up ahead,

ZIPPERMOUTH

the light changes to red. He hits the gas. "You are playing tonight," he sings knowingly, "without your husband, eh?" I sigh. I check the door to make sure its handle hasn't been removed, in case I need to jump out. This pot is making me so crazy that I can picture my own dismemberment beneath the Brooklyn Bridge, my headless torso rolling in the current, bumping gently against dock pilings, my rotting thigh reeled in by a fisherman. The driver stretches out his arm and roots around for something in the passenger seat, probably a gun. "Why a man he wants to be the woman?" he glowers, forehead glistening in the mirror. "And the other man, the one on top—" He raises his voice inquiringly, "The woman she is not tight enough for him?" He looks at me wide-eyed in the mirror, a humble naïf merely asking for information. I slide over on the seat to escape his line of sight and avert my gaze to look out the window, where a mattress careens past in the center of the street.

"I have to see you," Jane had said, calling five seconds after I'd walked through my door from a grueling day at *In Cold Type*. Shower, new Calvin Klein boxers, motorcycle boots. Tonight, I guess, lipstick. I've pursued a few girls; this is the luxurious part, when the friend thing begins to shift, slippage in the electrical impulses between you, waves start to oscillate in sync whether you know it or not, you're on the phone, say, discussing whatever, and halfway through, say, a character-assassination sentence about someone, you realize you've slid through some portal into a delicious game of anticipation, so surprising although expected that you might drag it out a bit to be sure and you half want it to go on forever but the tension's unbearable and finally unsustainable, you hit the tipping point and Jane calls like you knew she would: *Come over for Spaghettios and wine.* Pull on your '60s bell-bottoms and tight new gold lamé shirt with the ruffled collar from the thrift store and in a kind of soaring terror mixed with confident hysteria, fix your hair, do the lipstick with shaking hands, hop in a cab with a crazy fuckhead, hop out into the rockin' weekend streets, bound up the steps through the crazily tiled twin pillars adorning the portico of Jane's building, press the buzzer with your finger, Jane's finger presses back, the door clicks, you push through into the warmth of the hall, stride coolly up the marble stairs, knock knock, the door opens onto the swoony shock of her vivid face, steam behind her in the warm kitchen, over her shoulder lit candles on the table. Jane laughs, "Hi, get in here!" Turns to the shelf above the sink for a wineglass as you cross the threshold. "Are you drinking tonight or not?" While you're running the numbers, weighing the pros and cons, from the living room a voice. "What is up, foxy? Yay!" Look through the door and there on the multicolored vinyl couch is Damon. He laughs when he sees me, he looks happy. "Damon!" I exclaim delightedly. "High five, my brother!" Fuck.

Mom and Dad go to Las Vegas for the weekend. I'm seven. I wander from the house to a forbidden zone blocks away where the kids are strange. I'm not supposed to leave my own block except to play with Christy and her twin brother Kip across the street, but the territory beyond emits a magnetic pull and there's a babysitter in my house.

These kids are not friends with me and my friends. I don't know them from school. There are lots of them, swarming across a patchy lawn overgrown with dandelions gone to seed. I stand in the alley watching them, my ears buzzing from the power lines overhead. Beneath a clothesline some kid whose head is pale and big bends over a girl younger than me, maybe five, with short yellow curls, like Sally from *Dick and Jane*. Twilight greases his bare back. It's hot. In a garage next to me some of the big kids are clustered around. One of them has a bird in his hands, a tiny robin, not a baby anymore but not grown up either. I can't believe it. I spend whole afternoons in the backyard trying to chat telepathically with the sparrows bouncing about in the leaves of the ivy-covered fence, wondering if it's possible to stun one very lightly with a pebble and smuggle it into my room to be a pet. "Can I look?" I say to the boy holding the robin. He turns slightly toward me. "Don't touch it," he says, "because it's hurt." In his palm, the bird's miniscule beak opens and shuts. Just then the bigheaded kid from under the clothesline pushes me aside and joins the circle of boys, who close ranks and swallow the robin in their huddle. The humid air is aswirl with the smell of gasoline and dust. From the plank walls bike chains and fan belts dangle along with cobwebs festooned by moths struggling feebly in the afternoon heat. "What are you going to do with that bird?" I say to the wall of backs curved over the invisible creature. A kid with long oily hair looks over his shoulder. "We're going to operate."

I have a nurse's kit at home in my toy chest, in it is a stethoscope, syringe, and a bottle filled with multicolored candy pills. I used to take Anita Garner into the shed behind my house and give her shots, have her give them to me. It's indescribable, another person's hands sliding your pants down slightly, the plastic shot tickling your flesh, the dread of being caught by Mom at any moment. I'm dying to save the little bird. Maybe after the surgery I can tame it in my room. It could go outside whenever it wanted because I'll train it to fly back to me when I give the secret whistle. "Can I help in the operation?" I ask. These boys are old, maybe fifth grade;

they look at one another and shuffle. "If you come back really early tomorrow," someone says, "I guess maybe you could help. Anyway you can watch." For a second I see the robin in someone's palm turn its tiny head and blink.

It's impossible to sleep because in the morning they're going to operate on the little bird. I have sore throats and earaches all the time, soon I'll have a tonsillectomy, and tonight my eardrum in its cavern pulses with a thick swooshing ache. But Mrs. Stone the babysitter won't get me an aspirin because I'm "looking for attention." Through my bedroom door I watch her shape down the hall accumulate and dissipate, a large fish grimly adrift between living room and kitchen in the TV's watery flicker.

Everyone's still asleep when I lace up my tennis shoes, grab my nurse's kit, and sneak through the silent house just after dawn. Outside it's already hot. A scrawny cat rolls in the empty street. It's Sunday.

The yard, when I reach it, is deserted. Dust rises beneath my sneakers as I pace in the alley, staring at the closed door of the shack, nervous because the neighbors might be watching. Insects drone around a can of garbage. Finally I step up to the shed and try the door. It's unlocked. Inside the spidery darkness I stop to let my eyes adjust, nurse's kit hanging at my side. The air is a moist black cloth against my face but my throat is dry and my stomach feels as though someone's turning a screw into it very slowly. Even the wings are gone. I stand there for a minute, then turn around and walk outside. The spot under the clothesline where the little girl with yellow curls lay gazing up as the bigheaded kid leaned over her is just a patch of brown grass and gravel. Weeds along the garage make a rasping sound in the dry sluggish wind. I'm thinking, *What did they do with the head?* I move back inside and crouch down beside the robin's breast floating denuded as if shaved in its own red fluid in a pan. A feather or two drifts next to the small plump mound of flesh. It looks like a little turkey.

Outside in the white glare the world feels abandoned by people, as though an air-raid siren's gone off. The power lines buzz in my ears. When I reach Christy's house she's hopping around in the yard with Kip. We pull off our T-shirts to play Chinese jump rope in the driveway, hooking the elastic band around our ankles. Our flat chests glisten in the heat. When I get home, Mrs. Stone tells me everyone's been looking for me all day and that I'm in for a spanking when Mom and Dad get home, or at least she would hope so.

Dear Olivia, I'm sorry you had to see me OD like that when we were having such a good time! I don't know why I took all that dope. I guess the fistful of Valium impaired my judgment. It must've been terrible to see me lying on the floor all blue with the paramedics standing around and me making jokes about Elvis and Foucault. I guess it IS weird that I'm on Prozac AND Ritalin AND Valium AND heroin AND drunk! But I think it's good to write this down because it makes me realize how crazy I am. That my brain actually *needs drugs*!!

Hi Gia: I'm scared to tell you this because I'm scared you won't like me anymore. I can't believe I did this, but the other night at your house when you were taking photos of me as the Bee Princess I stole your Valium. Here we are, such good friends, the last person you'd think I'd steal from is you, but I did. When I saw the Valiums, I had to have them. I guess it wouldn't be such a big deal if the Valiums hadn't made me wake up crushed by depression. Because then I kept being depressed even after I'd taken Ritalin and drunk my morning coffee. So I took more Valium to get over the depression and went to work and told some jokes and hoped I'd feel better but for the whole three hours at work all I could think about was the remaining VALIUM, which I had to save because I was meeting Deano, Sanji, and Thalia for cocktails and since I didn't want to drink, the Valium was crucial. Thalia's that biologist/language poet/contact improvisation dancer whose brain is the size of France, who thinks I'm a total buffoon after that car wreck of a performance wherein something something, who even cares. I took the audience down a very dark path indeed, but anyway long story short I blacked out drinking shots of Jameson with Sanji, who's such a suave alcoholic she's practically James Bond. Anyway I'm really sorry I stole your Valiums. Because what ended up happening was I sort of overdosed after accidentally buying heroin and while I was in the hospital for two seconds I almost got you in trouble because I lied to Angel Grrl and Sydney and said you *gave* me the Valiums which I then had to take back because I didn't want to get you in trouble.

Dude, forget about the Valiums! It's my fault for leaving them around! Thanks for posing as the Bee Princess at the photo shoot. You looked insanely beautiful as usual & you're the best model ever. I'm in a shame spiral because Crystal French and I were higher than kites the whole session, like you didn't notice! Of *course* you took the Valiums. What are you—made of stone? And I just feel really bad because as you know we really support you in not drinking and smoking, though I have to admit it's been fun to drink and smoke with you in the past. Love, Gia

Hi Sydney. You're getting this in writing because (a) I'm drunk and (b) to let you know your friendship's literally a life-sustaining source of support, which of course is a nightmare of corniness! You must feel duped again and again. I know I used to feel like that when my dad professed remorse about his drunken actions only to turn up smashed in a restaurant hours, if not moments, later, facedown in a bowl of soup or sitting in his car on someone's lawn with the speedboat attached! You've listened to my expressions of remorse and rehabilitation repeatedly only to have them thrown up in your face when I get drunk. Not that I threw up in your face. I don't think.

Dear Angel Grrl. I'm sitting here drinking El Pico and staring at the sky which is the color of my LATE CAPITALIST RAGE. God I am SO FUCK-ING SORRY for screaming on the phone last night when you were so exhausted. It's just that my land-lady was driving me so fucking goddamn NUTS. Sometimes I get so selfish. I just didn't stop to think how on top of working these eighteen-hour days you're sick with that kidney infection PLUS you have to come home and walk Squid WHO'S SICK TOO so you have to clean up his diarrhea and vomit when you yourself are probably throw-ing up all over the place also! It was so selfish of me, pretending to ask you how you were doing when obviously I didn't care. But now that I've had a good night's sleep and a cup of delicious cof-fee, I DO care! I should've waited for my blinding rage to pass so I could call ONLY to check on YOU, knowing that I am nothing without my friends. I don't need to borrow money, either. Except for the three-block cab ride through these mean streets from your apartment back to mine. How I miss those heady days when we lay around in our boxer shorts snorting drugs and relaxing to *Crime of the Century* by Supertramp before we realized you were mature whereas I on the other hand was not only not mature, I was a lab rat in the basement of Bellevue, pushing the buzzer for more drugs until I exploded.

My new thing," I commented to Jane as we lay close together on the sand, "is I want to live someplace where when you look at the sky you feel glad you woke up."

"Totally," said Jane, shielding her eyes from the sun with a book. "Maybe the most important thing in life besides the people you love is to open your eyes to the sky."

"Like in Tucson," I said. "Where the sky is violet blue. Maybe lilac. Every day."

"Yeah," said Jane, eyes closed. Her hair was still damp from our swim. "For my nervous system, blueness spells a smile." She lowered the book over her face. A fat man wandered into the water, a small disfigured sea urchin in the waves. He listed and rolled in the teal surge like a Thanksgiving Day balloon. I snapped a photo. "Pliny thought there was a color, almost black, for which we have no name," I remarked, focusing on the man from a different angle. "That bastard," murmured

Jane. Idly her hand brushed over the sand, scooping it up, letting it run through her fingers, scooping it up. "Who the fuck was Pliny again?" she asked after a moment. "Some wino I knew in Tucson," I replied. "Because I think that color's called MY HEART!" Jane shouted, face still hidden by the book, which happened to be a gift from me. I'd loved the book so much I'd had a crush on it. For two weeks after I turned the last page the book lay on the floor next to my bed and whenever I looked at it I felt actual pain, so great was my sadness that the story was over.

A mammoth wave crashed down on the fat man's head and he disappeared. The horizon was tinted nearly the same shade as the sea. When a girl like me opens her eyes into a blue underwater morning, green feathery branches adrift like seaweed on the sky, I want that ultramarine to gather itself into a person. I would probably call her Jane, so I could bite her. The sun burned along my legs. I didn't mind my body when I was lying flat on my back. Jane's body next to me was beautiful. Her torso, designed for the palm of your hand. Tautly it swept down from the rib striations to her hip, begging my hand to rub circles across the tight warm skin of her abdomen, my fingers to pay attention to the hip bone, the delicate pulsing down there. I wanted to fuck her because it was difficult to imagine, occult. Down the beach families darted beneath their striped umbrellas and called out to each other in bright fragments, their voices gull cries or bits of colored glass.

Jane would undercut her own beauty sometimes by wearing unsightly vintage swimsuits. She could afford to be insouciant about what she wore. She was absorbing all the beauty of the seaside day, the sun the spray the sand, bringing it to a focal point inside her body, magnifying it exponentially to the point where she turned, trained her gaze on me, and burned my heart to a cinder. It bothered me to hear other people call her beautiful, say they loved her body. My heart would race and involuntarily my teeth began their grinding motion behind the smile I'd stretch across my face to hide my jealousy and indignation, imagining her nipple between my lips, a quick lick, the back of her neck in the palm of my hand, my mouth on hers, she kissing me with such nuance I'd never catch my breath. Who did she remind me of? On what molecular level did Jane set off that deep intracellular chime and clanging that kept me in this persistent shivery state, an ongoing electrocution? Vivien Leigh had green eyes and dark hair. More disturbingly, my mother's green eyes darted up maliciously, stung my consciousness, then vanished, leaving a tiny prick from which a thin fluid of revulsion and shame welled and began to spread. The green eyes of my mother, indeed. O harrowing thought, I have to kill myself right now.

10 Bonus Accomplishments of Today
1. Battled Satan
2. Didn't smoke pot (so far)
3. Swept floor, tied newspapers
4. Organized four files
5. Went to work in spite of spirit being broken on Rack of Menstrual Pain
6. Ate broccoli, "the colon's broom"
7. Endured lengthy conversation with X; faked waves of empathy
8. Didn't smoke for three hours after getting up
9. Walked to gym instead of taking cab
10. Celebrated diversity

I was reading Roland Barthes, hyped up on coffee and Ripped Force, a weight lifter's potion of ephedra and other herbal crystal meths, thinking of a girl sliding onto me, a girl not unlike Jane, shot through with distance and chill. The stereo played my new ambient love groove CD while images of an enormous tap-dancing cigarette pranced in my head. Roland said something like *photography, a new form of hallucination*, which got me worked up. It wasn't the meaning or anything; just certain words were green and lavender beads released from a cold capsule, pinging off my neurons to spark sensation. *Roland Barthes is beautiful*, I thought. *I love this song.* I loved it so much it made goose bumps on my arms and tears well in my eyes. Emotions and flickering half-ideas sluiced through me; thoughts began their swarm. Who else would love this song as much as I do, who can I hang out with who doesn't make me nauseous with boredom and simultaneous terror? Every few minutes the music and language and love scene in my head gathered into a wave of agitation so strong it propelled me from the chair. I'd wash a dish or two, make the bed, gather underwear from the stove, move my hairbrush away from the butter. I was trying to arrange a harmonious atmosphere conducive to creativity. To help myself, I'd bought the new CD, though spending the money had tortured me, in spite of my new pact with myself, my new rule: You are forbidden to worry or feel guilt about spending money on anything that a) facilitates your creativity, and b) isn't drugs. Or cigarettes or cocktails. Those pygmies sampled on the song really had a groove thing going on. I loved the little pygmies. I hoped I didn't have cancer. Not having a cigarette to suck into my lungs to help contain my emotions, to keep them within patrolable borders, was a nightmare. I couldn't focus. Nicotine deprivation revealed to me what a vacuum I was, what a suction machine of need and desire. God I love everything, I thought, gazing out my window at passersby several stories below. Blossoms dripping from the trees, robins in love warbling among the peeping spring budlets, trash spilling festively from an orange dumpster. I loved that Amazonian UPS driver bounding about in shorts; a girl I knew actually managed to seduce her after signing for a package. That emaciated visionary walking his mangy dogs beneath the ginkgo trees like he did every day in a paradigm-shattering costume of sandals and socks beneath an overstretched Speedo and bare rib cage—I worshipped him. The periwinkle sky and its cloud scallops arched up from behind the jumbled gothic architecture of rooftops across the street. I loved that shade of blue, what a sharp sensation it produced in my lungs! What chemical floodgate does a color open in your mind? Love leaked from my pituitary and converted on contact with my bloodstream into panic and I was swelling up, threatening to leave the ground and float off fast. I needed a cigarette, the tap-dancing kind, three feet long.

> Dear Judy Davis:
> Judy, as you know, I was born deficient in gamma-aminobutyric acid, or GABA, the neurotransmitter which modulates a person's anxiety response to the world. Without adequate GABA levels, I don't have to tell you, Judy, one is nothing BUT anxiety. After viewing you many, many times in such films as *My Brilliant Career* and the underrated *Naked Lunch* (I wish, Judy!), I realized that you, like me, are a GABA "undersecreter." Though you look so calm and composed in your films, Judy, I suspect this to be a well-rehearsed defense mechanism.

However, don't even TRY to tell me I'm the first person to respond to your telepathic cries for help, Judy! Acute perceptiveness, not egotism, is my curse. Though I'll admit I may be the first to recognize the seething sexuality kept so carefully in check by your commitment to professionalism and so-called Hollywood decorum.

I have to fine-tune my nervous system every day, Judy, with such medications as Prozac, to provide a base; Tegretol, an anti-epilepsy med designed to smooth those spiky brain waves and cut down on unexpected rage episodes; Ritalin, which helps me focus, supposedly; and finally, Xanax, which takes away the anxiety engendered by Ritalin, as I'm sure you know, since you're in the "biz," even though Ritalin is a lot smoother overall than the cocaine and other speed-like items I'm sure you and your so-called friends do quite a lot of to boost stamina on the set of your movies, not to mention at all those parties.

Though I have to say I don't picture you at so many parties, Judy, preferring instead to imagine you visiting a museum or sitting down to think about things in a park. A more accurate (and flattering!) portrait, I presume! Perhaps you are sitting on a park bench even now, constructing a memorable character in your head!

Judy, if you're like me, you've spent a good portion of your life adrift in the gloom of drawn curtains, captain of your own ship The Bed, taking along perhaps as passengers some potato chips and Coke. Perhaps like me you find yourself, Judy, glancing up from time to time to evaluate your naked body in the mirror on the ceiling, where sometimes what you see's okay, minutes later a catastrophe for which there are no words. So, what happened to your body in the brief interval between glances?

No doubt you, too, Judy, have felt yourself besieged by piles of books and the baleful glare of magazines, neither of which you can concentrate on for more than a few minutes at a time. You have felt swollen with toxins and harassed by the distant kitchen sink, populated as it is with turquoise bottles of vodka and their dregs, the garbage beneath clamoring with cigarette butts, their deadly silent cries disturbing none but you, Judy, and the plants, making their own terrible journey toward nightfall as you light more cigarettes to shock yourself from the dells of relaxation into which you occasionally lapse, your muscles sheathed in a film of anxiety, a constant apprehensive agitation beneath your skin having to do with hypochondria and lack of money, joblessness and dread of job, drug withdrawal, loss of love, whatever.

The body is a great thing, Judy, a horrifying thing, a great and horrifying thing to be trapped in a body, anything can go haywire at any moment, you're just hanging on with clenched teeth to a rope that swings your body sickeningly around and around over that bottomless and legendary thing we've come to identify as The Abyss.

Judy, when I saw you having sex with that insect in *Naked Lunch* I said to myself, "Here's a woman who thinks as I do." Judy, is there no end to your range, to the artistic risks you're willing to take? I realized that, like me, you must have been the daughter of an alcoholic, and that, during your teen years, you must have discovered, as I did, that the higher the level of alcohol in your cocktail glass, the lower the anxiety levels in your brain. Right?

On the upside, though, Judy, isn't it a relief to talk to someone who understands? I want to have my fist inside you, Judy, with you weeping the bitter tears of Petra von Kant. God, Judy, the insect. Your little cries! Judy, the sun is a whore.

Jane and I boiled hot dogs one sweltering afternoon before going for a swim. The city blazed with heat. Her apartment was such an inferno that even looking at the burner's gas flame threatened us with total personality disintegration. While we ate Jane read aloud from a how-to book on Christian ventriloquism written by a devout practitioner who called his puppet "the vent figure." Except for hot dogs our kitchens were bare of food, but happily Jane still had a can of El Pico so-called espresso, basically just pesticides dyed black, on a shelf above the stove. "I love a steaming delicious mug of formaldehyde during an ozone alert on a blistering day," I remarked. "That's when the magic happens," Jane replied. She stood and picked up a rabbit hand puppet lying next to a roach trap on the counter.

"I'm thinking of using this thing as the vent figure in my next naked stand-up routine, 'Tabletop Physics,'" she said. We grabbed our swimsuits and towels. On the landing she pulled the door shut, turned the key, and started down the stairs. "In Spanish, I believe *El Pico* means 'The Psychopath,'" she remarked, smiling at her evil landlord as we passed his apartment door, cracked open just wide enough to reveal his pervy eye.

Later, strolling home from the pool, I drowsily observed the current oscillating between our freshly rinsed auras. The dilapidated blocks had undergone a phase shift from zones combustible with violence to the sultry chiaroscuro of a black-and-white film starring Ava Gardner in a tropical setting. Cuernavaca, maybe. Or Uruguay. Around us the burning air banged with the usual honks, explosions, jackhammers, smashups, and shrieking brakes that were sometimes followed by the sick thump of a body landing inert on the pavement but now the din seemed faint, almost imaginary. In the air between Jane and me was poised a fundamental stillness so zingy and taut that it seemed you could accidentally have a thought shaped just right and the strung fabric of the day would stretch to form an opening contoured just like you, through which you'd step into Jane's hacienda—long lattices of dusk and sun falling from the blinds to spiral out beneath the fan blades and pass languidly across two damp swimsuits tossed on the chaise lounge at the foot of a bamboo bed, where the camera discovers Jane and me lying together entangled and disoriented, in shock at the downy warmth of the other's skin, so silky no matter where you touch, brush, stroke, or lightly trace a single fingertip along it in the shape of a tree, cloud, flower, cat, or sailboat. Of course you're both going to experience some respiratory distress.

"Let me draw you a bath," Jane said to my astonishment as we crossed from the fluorescence of the hallway into the dusky hush of her apartment. She disappeared into the bathroom and I heard the faucets start to gush. She moved back and forth between the bathroom and bedroom, hanging towels and doing Jane things while I stood in her living room, bolted to the floor. *Let me draw you a bath.* An apprehensive thrill started up in the clear channel running now between my solar plexus and the sacred dimensions of possibility, though another element lurked there as well, a faint breeze of suspicion, a hint of Fight or Flight. *Oh my god*, I thought. People didn't say things like that— in an unmistakably seductive and husky tone, parenthetically—by accident. *Let me draw you a bath*—it was Brontë-esque, was it not? Did I say that to Gia after a day of sensual delight spent half naked, cooling our burning bodies and splashing about in the aqua-tinted waters, then pulling ourselves, once cold enough, onto the glittering white deck tiled, in my memory, by vast granite blocks spangled with flecks of quartz and mica? Smoldering deliciously beside your companion, bodies infused with radiant heat from below and when it felt right you turned onto your stomach and it just went on like that. Now we're too hot, okay, let's jump in, now we're chilled, right on, let's jump out! Let's go have a cigarette, take a shower, jump in again, then do some yoga but act like we're not. Awesome! Did I do this with Gia or anyone else? Answer: No I did not. I certainly didn't invite someone home after a sexy fucking day of *jouissance. The infinitely transformative and playful properties of water as opposed to . . . A creative force much like an ongoing multiple girl orgasm, endlessly generative of possibility because . . . The liberation of consciousness from rigid and constricting hierarchies of . . . As exemplified by the eddies and swirls, the fall and shatter of water into emeralds the color of Jane's*—Jane reappeared from the bathroom to hand me a towel. "Take all the time you want," she said. "I'm going to call Damon and Terence to see if they want to come over for Spaghettios. Which they will buy."

How come Jane can't have a prosthetic limb belted beneath her skirt so she'd need me more than I need her?" I typed. "If only to bathe her stump?" I hit "send" and fired off the query to Gia during a lengthy email session masquerading half-assedly on my end as data entry. I couldn't be bothered to make any effort whatsoever in this way station of hell affectionately dubbed Dynamic Medical Pharmaceutical Catalogues. I rolled backward past the gray carpeted divider, my chair's misaligned wheels scraping over the concrete, and swiveled to scan the vast staging area of today's mission. I was tense with hunger and eyestrain. The building was some kind of hybrid warehouse/airplane hangar thing and a cell-shriveling glare bounced loudly from every surface but still the light felt murky. Things blurred out near the distant walls as though the air were infused with static. An electronic "oink" signaled that Gia's response had landed, and I turned back to my desk.

> I'm just sitting here looking at the *Letting Go* website and weeping about Emily though there's not much left of me physically after the so-called flu shot I received yesterday. First they opened up a layer of skin and muscle on my already weakened and quivering arm with an X-acto knife, then they took a high-powered Makita nail gun and shot it into the exposed and frightened nerve endings in my shoulder. Then they just said Fuck It and lopped the entire appendage off, then they fastened a piece of two-by-four to the jutting bone with an old cabinet hinge, and as if that wasn't enough, I

got the "flu" on the way home, I almost fainted, in fact I did faint, however not long enough to actually fall down and split my poor head on the dirty sidewalk, but long enough to have a vision of my life as it would have been if I were to remove all the negative synchronistic moments, like the time I was depressed back in the day and a friend who just happened to be there offered me a sample of heroin, which I then got addicted to and lived in misery for the next six years, and in a momentary recess from reality called "the faint" I saw myself planting an herb garden in New Bedford as a wooden screen door behind me squeaks open and slams shut behind a lovely young woman holding two mugs of steaming apple cider and looking a lot like Emily LeBuff . . . Whatever, I had a sad and psychic flu, but I realize I shouldn't be sad 'cause I'm actually living my dreams in a way, simply exchange New Bedford for rat-infested Chinatown, switch herb garden for piles of unpaid bills, replace the warm embrace of Emily with the ceaseless ring-a-ling of the phone, and SEE? The interchangeability of what should have been and what is, is complete! I'm psyched to see the book thingy we made, it was a smashup job you did as always, thanks again mein droog. Good luck on your performance next week. Try not to drink until right before you go onstage. Xoxoxo!!!!!

I finished reading the email, checked over my shoulder to make sure the Man wasn't bearing down on me, then hit "Reply."

G, with that missive you have proved conclusively that not only are you the most talented and insightful visual artist on the planet today, you are also the world's greatest living writer. Your prose leaves me breathless and panting for more. It delights even as it disturbs! With this in mind I am pleased to inform you that you are the recipient of the 1st Annual Lilah Plumjoy Creative Writing Fellowship for Excellence in Creative Writing. This entitles you to a lifetime scholarship to the writing workshops of Dr. Baby X and ensures that you will always carry the titles of Star Pupil and Teacher's Pet. Yes, the other students will envy you but that's their punishment for inflicting turgid prose "stylings" on the rest of us, their cloddish "sentences" which draw the reader forward as effectively as a giant bronzed German boot stuck in a bog exerting a cement-like influence around the trapped and anally laced ankle, a topic I explore in my forthcoming brochure, *Sentence to Nowhere*, which decries the impulse of today's youth to set their so-called Thoughts and Feelings down on paper. The same SUCKING sounds arise from their pages as from the deep impacted boot attempting to disengage itself from the bog much as the malpractising dentist attempts to dislodge the mischievous molar whose root snakes up through the cheekbones and behind the eyeballs into the frontal lobes where it provokes seizures too small to be categorized as such but which nonetheless ruin your life. I have to be on a panel and I think I'll call it *The Bad Day That Lasted Eleven Years*. For no reason. Thoughts? Still grappling with your remark

"I'm sitting here looking at January, and I just don't know what to do." Your assignment: pursue this story line about the harem harlots patrolling the streets of Dartmouth to harass people with tales of the arrival of Jolene. Just go with it.

We were watching a video in Jane's apartment. "Why don't you just throw her down?" Gia had said. "Obviously she's shy, she's a straight girl. They don't have a clue!" "She's not straight," I said. "She's just making boundaries or something." But tonight the pot was making me incautious and bold. Yeah, I thought. Why not? Someone had to make the first move. Had not Jane remarked to me just the other day that she had so-called "feelings for girls," and needed desperately to sleep with someone? This comment, delivered offhandedly as though to a casual friend rather than the person she flirted with mercilessly, had plunged me into confusion. But I refused to let on that I would ever interpret the remark as being in any way related to me. Rejection always wiped me out so thoroughly that I disappeared, leaving but a wrinkle in the air, it was too hard to reassemble myself after these annihilations. "Mm-hmm," I'd murmured in my most detached and clinical manner. "Yeah, sleeping with someone would sure be nice. Hmm."

On the other hand, was Jane's declaration not a hint of the most significant order, nay, a screaming cry for help? And was I myself not always eternally grateful when my opponent, whomever I was in love with at the moment, made the first move, breaching the moat of my passivity and terror of ridicule? Now I grabbed the bong and sucked in its smoke as though loading a cannon. "God, this is fabulous!" Jane shouted at the screen, where a French woman in a groundbreaking architectural hairdo and gown composed entirely of pearls dematerialized from a marble hallway and found herself time-warped into a garden, there to wander suddenly nude among naked statues. Was I swallowing my tongue? It was a cartoon in my mouth, difficult to locate. I moved it around and rubbed it against my teeth to make sure I controlled it, that it wouldn't slip down my throat. Jane swam next to me in the buzzing haze of my stony high; we drifted on the orange shag of the carpet, laughing and drinking the Flintstone jelly jars of red wine. Jane looked good in her jeans with the wide belt and tiny striped shirt. She'd cut her hair so it sliced across her forehead and curled behind her ear the way I liked. What would her neck smell like, there beneath her hair, behind the ear?

"Jane," I said.

"What," she said.

"Are we secretly smoking PCP?" The actors before

me morphed in their elegant clothes; my mind was a swamp heaving with green fog, or was it a twister of miniature vicious wasps, for sure it was a diffusion machine. This pot was strong. And Jane's hair was many, many things. Jane's hair was my lost adolescence, Jane's hair was a bottle of Suave Wildflower Shampoo, delicious at $1.99. Jane's hair was the cooing of a mourning dove, it was the call of the wild, Jane's hair was driving drunk at twilight with the Gun Club blasting "She's Like Heroin to Me," the roller-coaster hills of the rosy magic-hour road unrolling itself before you like your own enchanted destiny. Jane's hair was the gasp and melting sensation at the moment of first penetration during sex, it was anguish for a lost sweetheart, Jane's hair was a photograph of my mother holding me the day I was born, it was the sun just visible from the streaky window of a gas-station restroom, Jane's hair was a starfish, the stars, Jane's hair had a mind of its own. It whipped me back and forth in time, glossy supernatural vibes slithered down its strands and undulated over to coil around my neck. I was eleven, sitting in the padded cell of the family den watching Cher's variety hour on TV. Cher kindled in me a frantic longing that gave rise to a mild sensation of choking. As she sang "Dark Lady" in her Bob Mackie dress and flicked a black sheet of hair over her shoulder, using the back of her hand rather than her palm like everyone else, I grew drunk with love and found myself moved to compose an ode to her on one of my mother's recipe cards:

> Ocean Lady, dark and sweet,
> misty sea roar when she speaks,
> from the waves her green eyes swim . . .

But it never progressed beyond that. Suspended for all time, as though the poem were a fragment of ancient Greek verse on a pottery shard, was the issue of Cher's insectile disembodied eyes flung shoreward by the tide. My mother entered the room, sparks snapping from hair that convulsed and crackled like severed electrical wires, and an instinctive shame entered me, flashing through my limbs and causing me to shove the poem beneath my leg. When my mother left I tore the card in half, threw it on the grate in the fireplace, and torched it with a long match from the artful brass urn next to the Pres-to-Logs.

In the movie, the French actors posed beneath a dolorous male voice-over, remaining impassive even as they found themselves unmoored from the space-time continuum. Lost in contemplation, they roamed zombie-like through a maze of marble halls toward some unknowable destination, when without warning it was the day before and they were in the wrong bedroom, watching their lovers have cold sex with other emotionless guests. Jane smoked, gazing at the movie. The utter necessity and inevitability of our kiss filled the room, it was hard to believe she wasn't moving toward me of her own accord, hard to believe the kiss hadn't in fact already happened. "Hey, Jane," I said. She turned her head toward me. "Jane," I said, feeling light-headed, "um, maybe you should slide over here and . . . " Shock flashed across her face and I stopped. "Uh-oh," I said.

Quickly Jane's features recomposed themselves into a sweet, slightly chastising smile. Was that a hint of disappointment beneath her surprise? Suddenly I understood that I had violated some understanding between us, a wordless trust. I laughed. "Okay, okay, I'm sorry!" I yelled. Jane shook her head. "Was that necessary?" she asked gently. "It's not me," I begged. "It's the pot. Marijuana's a ventriloquist and I'm the vent figure." Not looking at me, Jane laughed. "Pot's an evil junta and I'm its puppet dictator," I gasped. I couldn't breathe. Smiling, Jane stubbed out her cigarette and reached for another. "I always enjoy the concept of the 'junta,'" she remarked, lighting up. "Hoonta," she mused, blowing smoke rings. "Hoonta."

My heart knocked against my ribs. We resumed focus on the movie. "I have to kill myself right now," I said, after a moment. "Relax," said Jane. "Shit," I said.

"Fuck." I crossed my arms on my chest and stared at the TV. Which I couldn't see. The sizzling highway of humiliation unfurled before me, the delectable green of my stony haze burning off along the roadside, asphalt turning crimson beneath the onrush of bloodred shame. Here is my body, a construct of blood and pistons pumping, a shame machine. I'm not myself, I am a sheep. "Jane, I'm so sorry," I said. "Why did I say that? I don't know why I said that."

"Shut up!" shouted Jane. "It's okay." "Oh my god," I said. "Oh my god." Onscreen a pack of rabid reporters in suits nipped and yelped at the actress. "Do you sleep in pajamas or a nightgown?" barked one wearing glasses with thick black frames. "Neither," she breathed languidly, throwing her arms back and tossing her leonine head on a chaise lounge. "I sleep only een two drops of Fransh parfoom."

"I cannot cope with her genius," said Jane. "Should we open another bottle of wine?" I said. "Good thinking," Jane replied. She stood, drained her jelly jar, and headed for the kitchen. My eyes remained fixed on the flirtatious movie star burbling and wriggling on the chaise. "She's so far out of her mind she's back in it!" Jane shouted happily, skewering the cork from a bottle of Merlot.

Cat hairs clogged my nostrils with each breath. The tattered black velvet cloth over the window flapped lightly with a breeze along its edges and shadows scuttled about the walls. My comforter had escaped its cover to bunch and tangle with clothes discarded at the foot of the bed. An enormous stack of videos teetered on the dresser next to the TV and Cherry sprawled against me, lying on her side, curled paws kneading the air as Steve licked and bit her ear, paw pressed against her neck. Suddenly it occurred to me that today I was supposed to be taking some sort of test. I closed my eyes, then opened them. Ragged borders outlined flesh-colored territories on the ceiling where paint chips peeled off each night to rain on my head. What test? The glass thing shielding the light bulbs was black with a thick silt of decomposing moth wings, flies, and baby roaches. Fine. Lying on my wicked pallet I begged the ceiling to dissolve into shimmering miasma, release a vision of pestilence and snakes, redeem the mundane yet hideous reality of this morning in shrieking delirium. What fucking test? In what banal way with nonetheless enormous consequences was I about to fuck up today? A tiny collective screaming started somewhere way down in the abused mouths of my molecules; only dogs could hear it but I felt its thin vibration globally beneath my skin. I ran a mental inventory of my kitchen cupboard, trying to remember if I had any Nyquil, Benadryl, Advil, whatever worthless OTC shit, anything to help me get back to sleep. I tried to roll over but my leg seemed to be stuck. I pushed the wadded bedclothes away and looked down to find my calf cemented to the mattress by some sort of amber substance. God, had I stabbed myself? The horror registered in my lungs as an abrupt sense of compression before my brain had even begun to apprehend the debris-field of styrofoam containers in which I lay. French-fry cartons and minute foil-covered tubs of syrup festooned the room, a half-eaten pancake on the rug. Lovely.

The phone rang. The machine picked up and beeped, followed by a sinister pause. I waited. Labored breathing chuffed from the speaker, signaling a call from Lepa, my ancient diabetic landlady, owner of every building on my block. Invariably she waited before speaking, as though peering through the wire, her crafty periscope rising from the phone to swivel in search of my cowering form. "Renting!" she shouted in an Eastern European accent. She couldn't remember my name so she called me "Renting." "Renting! Why you no pay the rent?" Another pause, filled with wheezing and mumbles. "Why you no call me back? I call to you three times." I pulled the pillow over my head. "What kind of girl you no pay the rent? Always before you paying the rent! What happened to you?" She sounded sad. "Okay. Calling me back, please, or I go to the lawyer." Another gasping silence, then she hung up.

I stared into the darkness of the pillow. What kind of girl, indeed.

"Fuck it," I said, jumping from the bed. The pain of my leg hair ripping from the maple cement felt good. I turned the TV off. "I need a toasted bagel with cream cheese and some coffee," I announced to the cats. Excited, I shot downstairs to the curb; through the gray nimbus of my headache I could just make out the bagel place across the street. I felt in my pocket and came up with nothing but change. I didn't get paid for three days. Spinning blades of light glanced from my eyeballs, the metallic cacophony of brake drums and gears and engines drilled into my ears. Rageaholics veered toward me. When I finally stormed into the store, exhausted, I ordered a bagel with tomato and onion from the Chinese guy. Fuck it. I was hungover and living large, getting me a motherfucking bagel cuz my life a piece of shit. Not my life is a piece of shit. Just my life, no verb, piece of shit. My life a piece of shit. These and other thoughts related to the grammar and syntax of the existential bind whirled laboriously through my mind as I made my request and passed my change across the counter.

The Chinese guy smiled and nodded approvingly, saying "Oh yes, oh yes," as though mine were the most sensible order he'd ever heard. And, I reflected, it was. The order was honest, that's what it was. *We are imprisoned in a society of lies*, I reminded myself. Gratefully I smiled at the guy and, taking the warm bundle, made my way back across the vast avenue and returned upstairs to discover a bagel coated with cream cheese and, rather than tomato and onion, grape jelly. *Shit*, I said. Fuck *me*. My eyes filled with tears. The bagel place was too far away, it was in a different country, I couldn't go back. I'd spent all my strength on the stairs. I sank down on the bed. This my life it = suckage. Moments later a wave of hatred and rage flung me like a demon from the bed, and I found myself propelled back across the treacherous street to the store. Politely I reported the catastrophe but with an edge in my voice. "No problem," the guy said cheerfully as he made the new one. "Crazy jelly," he hummed. "For you crazy jelly, no problem at all." This fucking city. Twinkling, he gave me the bagel with tomato and onion and the jelly bagel too as a bonus and I came home and ate them both, staring balefully at the wall. Should I go back to bed? The phone rang. I reached over to raise the volume on the machine. Make it worse, Satan, I dare you. ". . . two forms of ID to prove you are . . ." A fist of terror began to accrue in my stomach. I felt vertiginous, my eyes were dry and stinging. I turned down the sound. Wait. I crumpled the paper bag and stood up from my chair. Hadn't I bought dope? My hangover was strictly alcoholic. *Had* I bought dope? Where was the dope? Frantically I felt in my pockets. Moving to the bedroom, I checked the nightstand, yanked my pillow from the bed, lifted the pancake on the floor. Steve and Cherry sat side by side at the stove, regarding me with interest. I had to think. What had I done last night? I'd hit the bank with three dollars in my pocket, left with forty-three. Spent five dollars, probably, at McDonald's. Okay ten, what did I know. That left enough for three bags of heroin. Maybe the envelopes had fallen from the pocket of my shirt when I'd tossed it on the table. I dropped to my hands and knees and commenced a sweep of the apartment. Delighted, the cats trotted for their toys. Steve pranced up on his hind legs, juggling a catnip hamster. "No one gets to party," I said grimly, cheek on the tile, hand waving beneath the stove, "until we find the drugs." The phone rang again.

"Goddamn it," I shouted, standing and looking wildly around. The cats scrabbled across the floor and disappeared. Now I remembered what the test was, actually a battery of tests. I'd scheduled an appointment with a new agency, *Temps and Plus*. My ribs felt like they might crack from the pressure in my chest.

I jerked open a drawer, pulled out the hammer, and slammed it down on my answering machine. A growling noise scratched past the back of my throat. I kicked the machine across the floor; above it, hundreds of dishes, though as far as I knew I only owned five or six, encrusted with food I didn't remember eating, spilled across the counter. My glance skidded past the mirror and my reflection. I hoped this was what was known as "snapping"; I wanted to snap. In a very deep way I felt the need to come unglued. I was too sensitive for this evil world; I wanted a genteel nervous breakdown. I needed a diagnosis. I wanted understanding orderlies with a stretcher and calming drugs, cold cloth on my forehead, and a rug across my lap while I gazed moodily from the sanitarium deck across the magnificent Maine coastline. Though now, looking at the hammer in my hand and the shattered remnants of my answering machine, I felt depressingly sane and embarrassed. I dropped the hammer. My emotions were huge but they refused to rip me away from my superego overlord, blind me to the consequences of my actions. I slugged my thigh. That was sort of satisfying, so I did it again, but not too hard.

In my dream an ugly little monster toddled across the porch of a dilapidated brick row house to an ancient hag in a rocking chair. "Are you my muhver?" he asked, tugging at her greasy skirt. The malevolent crone kicked him away and continued to rock, her empty eye sockets trained on the distant horizon of factories and shattered glass glittering in empty lots. The mutant toadlet spun from the blow and bounced like a windup toy against my legs. Looking up at me with confused eyes, he said again, "Are you my muhver?" I realized at once that his mother, ashamed of her grotesque offspring, had abandoned him to continue motoring in her Corvette to cocktail parties, where she and her fellow thespians conspired about their upcoming production of Ibsen's *A Doll's House* at the local community theater. She planned to inhabit the role of Nora with a level of nuance that many would consider supernatural. Having just learned to walk when his mother pushed him from the car's open passenger door and sped off, the suckling eyesore wandered in his diaper and striped shirt for many days until he landed here, on the poor side of town, where skeletons with fur that some called dogs dragged themselves along, heartbreak oozing from the sores devouring their skin. One of these animals had taken the hideous nursling under her paw, and the two crawled together through the dirt, the dog sniffing for cigarette butts to feed the baby since her melancholy teats were dry. Most of the tot's baby teeth jutted through holes in his harelip, so naturally he spoke with a lisp.

"Hew name ith Wuff," he explained to me, petting the friendly mutt until his finger stumps were sticky with her pus.

Trying to wag her tail, Wuff tipped over. Shunned and lonely, the infant freak wanted only to take his nap, but he was too short to climb into bed. Unbearably sad for the exiled beastling with his mop of troll hair, I picked him up, ripping several muscles in my neck, for he was super dense, but clutching him to my chest I staggered to his closet between two tar-paper shacks. Wuff dragged herself along beside us. The tiny lair was long and dark and filled nearly to the top with newspapers balled up as in a fireplace. I placed the squat and scabby cub like a log onto the wadded tabloids; then gently, so as not to shatter her, I raised Wuff's weightless frame and lowered the kindling of her bones next to her little friend. Wuff winced. She raised her sweet brown eyes to mine despairingly and twitched her muzzle slightly, as though to whimper a request or explanation, but she was too weak. I heard her in my mind, though, for we had a wordless understanding.

Woof woof, Wuff, I reassured her silently, using my telepathic powers. I pulled my shirt off, placed it over the paper, and shifted Wuff onto the soft cloth. Relieved of the caustic burn against her hide, Wuff nuzzled the soft cheek of her new charge, who snuggled in, wrap-

ping his chubby tentacles around the dog's neck. A pin-
point of light winked from a diamond or crystal goblet
behind my little friends. Oh that's nice, I thought,
before realizing with terror that the light was a spark.
In the crypt's back wall a ratty window frame ignited,
spreading at once to the newsprint.

"Fire!" I screamed, a cry masking the sound of red-
hot pincers shredding my back muscles as I lifted the
leaden tadpole and tossed him to the porch before grab-
bing Wuff, whose sores had begun to sizzle. Though the
mutant fledgling crashed like a solid uranium cannon-
ball through the rotted boards to the dirt below, still he
and Wuff gazed up at me with a love I felt could destroy
me, a love I craved and returned. I had rescued a newborn ogre from his tinderbox crib and now prepared
myself with immense tenderness and joy to meet the
challenges of motherhood but then I panicked—how
would I care for my helpless little gargoyle and Wuff, I
had no money!

"Everyone in your dreams is an aspect of yourself,"
my therapist had once remarked smugly, taking the
easy way out.

I burned down to a sputter as we sucked our breath in
together. A few rays of sunlight filtered through the
lowered blinds. This was love. August blew through the

window in sheets and curtains of burning soot, gaseous exhalations, fumy liquids. You tried to hold your breath walking in the streets.

Jane floated beside me on the punitive mattress in my darkened bedroom. The buoyant dope drift disguised my unyielding bed's ill intent toward the human form. After a while she rose to go throw up. She couldn't stand having her face in the toilet so she threw up in the tub, running water so you wouldn't have to listen. Sometimes she couldn't make it to the bathroom and retched over the kitchen sink, faucets blasting. "Oh my god." She collapsed on the bed. "You okay?" I whispered. "God, yes," she said, "I'm great. I don't mind throwing up when I'm this high." "Evidently not," I murmured, drifting off.

After the first rushes of ecstatic conversation, Jane and I wandered from room to room, speaking occasionally in undertones. We were specters facing each other through soundproof glass, semaphoring unintelligibly. Langorously we'd drape ourselves across the bed, a chair. Puking occurred in slow motion. She may as well have kicked me in the teeth when she lay down with her feet on the pillow next to my face, her head way down there as far away from my mouth as she could get, and this cruelty made me crazy with love. I had no expectations when we got on the bed, well maybe I did, perhaps in fact I was absolutely distraught with involuntary anticipation, but anyway no one was safer now from unwanted advances than Jane.

Beneath my blithe exterior, of course, I seethed with fury and confusion. *Dear Universe: She's the one who started flirting first, goddamn it.* I'd known she was straight and when we first met I hadn't even considered the notion of pursuing her until she opened the door that night on the sidewalk, coyly reciting her dream parable about being stranded on the mountain above Damon and me. But now with Jane beside me on the bed or anywhere, I was totally cool, I was so cool I was beyond good and evil. I wore the beret of coolness at a rakish angle on my head. I snapped my fingers with my coolness. I didn't give a shit and all you motherfuckers can eat me.

In the detox the first thing the admissions nurse did was take me into a closet and, without looking me in the eye, request that I pull my pants and underwear down "all the way to your ankles," and squat before her. Humiliation jolted through me as though from a cattle prod. She held a clipboard, pencil poised. I realized she wanted to see if I was smuggling bags of dope in my lady parts. My heart banged against my rib cage and various scenes from women-in-prison movies flitted through my head—was she going to perform a *cavity search*? My twattage a crime scene, the first fingers inside it since whenever not heavenly and ardent but forensic, rummaging for evidence of my indolence and its companion, crystalline poppy in a packet. But she made no move toward me. I guess she wanted to see if the tiny envelopes would come shooting out when I bent my knees. I was enraged she would suspect me of this subterfuge. Why would I bring dope when I'd entered this hellhole voluntarily? I had placed myself before her, asked her for help against myself. Opiates bisect you so cleanly down the middle that one part of you can check into detox quite easily while the other part, your evil twin, is busy stuffing bags of dope into your vaginal "vault," as my disgusting gynecologist called it. In my considered opinion I personally hadn't sunk that low yet but if I continued down this dark path it was just a matter of time before my sporadic but regular binges transformed me into a hungry ghost condemned to wander an overlit freeway of eternal craving, everybody said so.

This nurse must have seen every ruse in the book. I wasn't like the other wretches who checked in here, of course, but she couldn't know this. I smiled to help her feel more comfortable, to clue her in that I knew she must hate performing this tiresome little pageant with patient after canny patient, and that I appreciated she was enduring it for my own good. She must be so bitter about her assignment to these grim environs, surely no one volunteered to man the detox. I smiled at her as I squatted in the cold closet so she could see that I myself recognized the absurdity of the roles we both played. I wanted her to understand that I wasn't angry, I didn't hold her personally responsible, I knew this gruesome tableau was simply one of her duties though almost certainly one omitted from her job description by those bastards in HR who had therefore ambushed and demeaned her just as she was now forced to ambush and demean me and, most crucial of all, I needed to impress upon her that I realized it was my own fault I found myself in this situation. I was sure quite a few addicts flipped out when she asked them to pull their pants down and squat. Probably envelopes of dope did come shooting out of their nether parts. Not me. No dope shot out and I was a model of graciousness and self-composure. I remembered my mother telling me whenever humiliating things would happen at the doctor, like rectal thermometers, shots in the ass, my first Pap smear, etc., that doctors saw these things every day, they didn't even notice. Your secret area was like an electric can opener to them, just another appliance to check for defects. I grabbed this thought from the thousands babbling panic stricken in my brain as I pushed my jeans, then, after hesitating, my orange-and-blue-striped boxers, down to my knees. The nurse called my underwear "panties." For some reason this was so upsetting that even now I can barely write it down. It was an ugly word, I couldn't figure out why. It made me want to black out, seal my ears, have my eyes sewn shut. So many words can make you want to die. "Pull your panties down to your knees and squat," she said, pencil poised above her clipboard. I closed my eyes and smiled. "Squat" itself is a vulgar term. It must be so painful for her to say several times a day. *Pull your panties down and squat.* She took all my books away, in case drugs were hidden in the pages or spine, and all my clothing, except for some psychedelic underwear and socks. I suspected she might grant me bonus points for my eclectic taste in vibrant hues. She had me undress and gave me paper slippers, pajamas, and a thin blue robe. When I left the room, clutching my remaining paper bag of possessions to my chest, I thanked her humbly. I felt sorry I'd put her in this position.

Now Jane's body drifted next to mine on the bed. The bed bucked and spun in a muffled kind of way and Jane whirled beside me in our private tornado, her hair a mess her eyes closed, all fucked up and Oh My God. In lieu of touching one another, we snorted lines of dope. The nurse was right. The tiny packet of dope had replaced my libido; in its place was a plastic envelope stamped *Black Widow* or *911* or *X-Press.* Put your hand inside me, and your fingers would freeze in the numbing powder. Hearts pounding, Jane and I leaned across the mirror with a straw and sucked it up. We smiled at one another and left our bodies, laughing with relief. We would snort the dope and vacate our bodies, leaving shells awash in the gentle slosh and whistle of our organs.

Emerging from the subway into the miasma of workers, men striding superbly in their splendid suits, streaming currents of thick-headedness and cologne, ripe to bursting with generalized contempt, lost in thought no doubt of cigars growing cold on their tongues, the snaky veil of aggression and self-defense filming their eyeballs behind which circulated thoughts like *Should I buy a speedboat or what?*, the usual shock of cognitive dissonance hit me when I realized that many of them were at least seven years younger than me. I thought I was walking alongside versions of my dad, strong-smelling, utterly unself-conscious and middle-aged. But their smooth white skin and cherry cheeks gave them away. It's like these kids woke up in their little spaceship pajamas and stepped into the paradigm of successful manhood standing like an open sarcophagus next to the bed, an animatronic container for their lives. It was a tight fit, though, and a force field repelled anything that might gum up the works, so when the door swung closed there was always a bit of ectoplasm left behind on the sheets. I felt bad for them. I headed for the museum, gasping for breath in the sea of worker garments, the snickering tangerine suits on the women, the judgmental black jackets, the blast of frustration from a pseudo-psychedelic scarf, the vicious and frantic click of spiked heels on the sidewalk. Some lady turned toward me, a plastic and velvet parrot appliqué on her sweatshirt, the visual equivalent of a mallet in the face. We reached the curb and I waited in the swell of colors and perfume for the light to change.

Look both ways, step from the curb, and have the following thought as you stumble through the cross-walk: seventeen dollars until Thursday. Passersby make their way through the hardening cement of the work-day. I fought the impulse to kneel on the asphalt cow-ering, arms protecting my head. I don't care, it's fine, everything's fine. Focus on the body's tiny incessant needs. I was cultured and grown on a small planetoid, my physiology dependent on the corrupt chemical com-pounds of the biosphere, so I stole a banana. Decided it was okay since the checkout girl was Satan. I'm trying to heal the world one soul-crushed cashier at a time so I was nice and in return she was a cunt. I glanced over at the God Bless America Nail, Tanning, and Hair Salon, its sign painted in giant flowery script. Next door, steps descended from the street to the cheery little busi-ness Crafts & Talk. I searched in vain behind the plate glass for a glimpse of ladies knitting and chatting at a table, which of course is what the sign would lead you to expect, and their absence never failed to sadden me. Fourteenth Street in winter, cold and windy, the flinty white sidewalk and its glare, sunlight bouncing from the surface in shrapnel that struck your eyes hard. In summer it was more liquid and melty, like now. At what point did the clacking beaks of death birds start poking up through the sewer grates? During flood season in the Amazon, fish swim among the upper branches of the canopy. *The law of the diagram is that one starts with a figurative form, the diagram intervenes and from the scramble a form emerges, or a form scrambles forth from the diagram, disfigured, called the Figure.*

For years my body ambulated through the grid, chewing things up, devouring, almost always in a state of panic. Places I have gone on my own two legs, swinging them across the sidewalk, the bricks towering around me feel like they're inside my skin, abrading me from within—is there no way out of this equation? Jane gave me a book which I haven't read yet, but when I opened it up I saw "Deglaze with your bone water, reduce, repeat. Glutamic acid is tasteless." Was there anything good in my desire for Jane? Was there real love? I mean, did I really care about Jane and want the best for her, or did I just want to suck her blood? Places I have gone: across the avenues to score drugs at all times of the day and night; to work and home from work in a cab or on a bike, subway, bus; to the check-cashing place, to bookstores, thrift stores, and libraries; to get my hair cut and colored; to nightclubs and the apartments of girls I'm in love with who don't love me back, of girls smitten with me and rejected by me, without grace. Monkeys become ducks when the Amazon floods, fish feed on fruits, river dolphins race through the treetops though yesterday their leaves brushed against the moon—that's what I wanted to say. Crabs clacking in the canopy that yesterday soared into space, leaves rustling against the moon. Now in the crosswalk the air around me hemorrhaged neon from the skirts and blouses of the workers, lifting me on its surge. I felt nauseous. I felt faint. I wanted Jane. I wanted Jane walking beside me, chain-smoking after yoga, Jane of the striated muscles and psychotic clothing, attire of humor and madness.

Not long ago, following a ghastly night together of cocaine panic attacks with no heroin to calm us down, either because it wasn't available or we were being good, probably the former, Jane bounded from the bed after approximately eight minutes of a fitful, fibrillating sleep. She had to catch a cab to the airport, she was meeting friends in Jamaica, it was cheap this time of year, and she cried, "God, I'm hungover. I was so lonely and *sad* in the bed! Should I wear all red on the plane?"

I too had been lonely and sad, nay miserable, out

 ZIPPER MOUTH

here on the vinyl couch. I had been isolated and afraid as my heart galloped against my esophagus and the mistreated dog in the apartment below wept into the air shaft outside Jane's kitchen window. We had retired the snorting equipment around 4 a.m. and the clock inched toward 4:30 then 5 after Jane abandoned me for the bedroom and I lay on the couch, the movement of the clock hands measured according to the number per minute of my accelerated heartbeats while the dog's despondent tune slid up the bricks and through the window screen, gliding along the carpet and over the couch cushions into my ears to pool behind my eyes, stuck. I couldn't cry but if I ever did they would be the tears of a dog. I drank beer after beer from the six-pack on the carpet to try and choke down fear, listening to Jane toss and cough in the bedroom, and now I wanted to say, "Well if you were so lonely and sad, Jane, why didn't you have me come and get into bed with you?" But of course I couldn't say this, I reasoned, because if she'd wanted me in the bed, she would certainly have asked. Jane knew that at any given moment all she had to do was utter the command and I was at her service. On the other hand, perhaps that wasn't the problem at all: maybe she was trying to tell me now that she'd *wanted* me in the bed but had been too shy to ask. As if. The crushing fact was that Jane was lonely and sad *in spite of my presence.*

On the other hand, I reflected, as she searched frantically for her wallet, Jane could have been commenting simply on the horrors cocaine visited upon your brain chemistry, taking you to an arid, skeletal place of abandonment and despair, a Burroughsian Place of Dead Roads that existed entirely independent of your life circumstance, a place to be found exclusively at the bottom of a cocaine spiral, a place always and only purely chemical. I stood in the living room locked in sadness while Jane rushed around pushing things into a cheap nylon bag. I loved the orange bag, shaped like a sausage, that Jane was stuffing. Loved Jane for knowing one could go out and purchase an orange nylon bag in which to tote your belongings. It was always this way for me: each time the beloved showed they could do any ordinary task in the real world, something anybody on earth did every day as a matter of course, it deepened their mystery for me and made me crazy with love. I would be stabbed with love and admiration to the point of collapse. For I was not like them, these doers of the ordinary. Invariably, it never occurred to me until the moment of departure that one of the salient characteristics of the journey was the travel bag or suitcase; until it came time for actual packing, the concept of the suitcase never crossed my mind. Consequently the packing frenzy in the hour prior to leaving for the airport always consisted of me shoving my entire apartment into a ridiculously heavy ancient bag with a broken handle, a remnant of some long-ago excursion to a Salvation Army. The suitcase was always jammed to bursting with outfits for the vast spectrum of glittering social events I was sure to attend. Hair products leaking onto books, illicit pills and vitamins, eye shadow, lip liner, skin repair products—everything necessary for a total makeover. Highlighters, pens, scissors, notebooks, and photos for the many projects I was sure to initiate once free of my vortex of mental illness and poverty. Envelopes for the numerous letters I planned to write and never did. Stacks of bills which I somehow imagined being able to pay with the cash sure to materialize in the magic zone of my destination. When the suitcase was fully jammed and had to be unpacked again to get it to close, I always vowed to get a really good bag first thing when I returned and when I returned from the trip I always forgot about suitcases entirely until the next frenzied hour before departure.

Jane zipped up her bag then reached into my backpack and pulled out a book. "I need this for the plane," she said. When she was ready to go, I was thinking of kissing her in spite of the iron vibrations that shook my hungover frame—I felt electrocuted, rusting, weepy. When Jane was ready she put on a bright red pair of pants and a soft red threadbare T-shirt, the shirt a paler shade of red but in the same family of reds as the pants which were a cheap wrinkled cotton. Jane's green eyes with their black fringe were practically swollen shut, her skin was mottled from our night of terror, and her spiky tomcat pelt shot into many conflicting directions and never had she looked more beautiful to me as she swiped some lipstick across her mouth, lips so glamorous and poignant in her desperate and humorous hungover face. I couldn't believe she was going to Jamaica, I couldn't believe she could *walk*. But she bounded to the sidewalk with her sausage-shaped bag, there was a hole in the seat of her red red pants, she turned at the curb and blew me a kiss, flowed into a cab, and was gone.

I reached the end of the crosswalk and was swept up to the sidewalk with the crowd. I was smoking a cig across the street from the Metropolitan Museum, each cell in my body buzzed, a microscopic wasp. White dress with black polka dots and art earrings, combat boots, purple eye shadow. Skirt blows up. Sometimes I kind of like it, but cellulite—where was Jane? Hot out, breezy, blue sky: gray buildings stacked all around, fortresses of wealth. Suddenly Jane materialized in the crowd across the street, stepped to the curb, and lit a cigarette.

Times You Have Touched Me

1. Showing me how to do a yoga stretch. I was standing up and you placed your palm on the back of my neck, the tip of your finger at the end of my tailbone. Imagine my surprise. "It's okay," you murmured. "Just relax." I held my breath. "It's just a technique," I told myself, "not an emotion." Gently you bent my spine forward and my vertebrae sizzled and went up in a puff of smoke where you touched it.

2. There are no other times. Except for that incident wherein you applied some cherry color to my lips. We were dressed in matching outfits for some trip to the disco and I'd forgotten my lipstick. "Here," you said. "Try this new color." You wore black eyeliner and leaned in, raised your arm to my face. Impulsively I said, "Put your whole hand inside." You laughed. You held my head and stroked the red stick against my lips.

3. That's a lie. I was sliding lipstick across another girl's lips at some dance thing, a sexy girl to be sure. I liked flirting though she made me nervous. "Put your whole hand in my mouth," she said, and I laughed. Do I wish I'd said that to Jane or not?

As we walked down the black sticky streets past scarred brick tenements, the boarded-up windows of the former telephone building, homeless people muttering and smoking in their soggy cardboard clubhouses beneath the scaffolding on Thirteenth Street, an avenue of hell jutting through the membrane of another dimension into this one, where Jane and I walked, our arms slick in our tank tops with the foul hot steam rising from the asphalt, Jane wondered how I was and I reported really great, thanks, that I suffered from a lot of disturbing random thoughts but otherwise I was pretty okay, actually, after two weeks without drugs, and Jane laughed and said, "Well that party's about to come to a screeching halt."

An anxious wind rattled my interior. Butterflies of black adrenaline rushed and fluttered in my stomach and dread inflated my upper arms and ran through my knees. The first day without drugs two weeks ago had passed slowly as though it were a pool of cold tar and I a thing being extracted with forceps. I lay on my bed in the dark for eons while the manic toxins grumbled inside me and the stench of unchanged cat litter settled across my face like a shroud. The landlady knocked on my door, shouting for the rent, then the super, same deal, then the landlady again, then the gas man while I held my breath. On my bed, surrounded by the Gatorade, Cheetos, and Jack Daniels I needed to ease withdrawal, simple normalcy seemed as distant and magic and encircled in haze as I don't know what.

"Oh, please," Jane said with exasperation, noticing my expression. "We're already bombed. C'mon. We'll

 ZIPPER MOUTH

do the tiniest amount. Just enough to take the edge off." I smiled. I stared again into the gaping throat of that first drug-free day. In the air shaft pigeons cooed and footsteps passed up and down the stairs outside my apartment. People jingled their keys, Steve and Cherry romped in the kitchen. Voices drifted up from the sidewalk, people laughing, the sounds of summer in the city. Perhaps they were running out for iced coffee, or going to a matinee. I couldn't even make it to the shower. The bedroom doorway burned vermilion in the glow of afternoon sunlight heating the living-room windows. I watched the cats, tumbling through a rosy haze. I recalled the excitement of tying new sneakers, age six. Being young, one jumped from the bed because, well, yellow slices of sun, yellow sun sliding down, a thick yellow paint swath of sun in the sky.

"When we wake up we'll go to the gym for a steam. I'll buy us a cab," Jane said. "Look, it's okay even if we OD, because I have health insurance now!"

We laughed. I leaned against a wall. I tried to think. "Aarggh," I said. Jane's body was not my body—she would leap from the bed tomorrow and be smoking and drinking with good cheer by twilight. I looked to the heavens and rolled my head back and forth against the bricks. "Do you have low blood sugar or something?" Jane asked. "Did you eat?" She pulled a compact from her little purse. "Yes. I had fifty Manhattans, remember?" I said. "With cherries. Help me please, Random Deity. Fuck." I rolled my head some more. "Jane, I gotta go." She rubbed powder on the sponge and stroked it across my forehead. "We don't have to do this," she said. "I'm being selfish." She swept the powder down my nose and cheeks, dabbed above my lip. "I just missed you and wanted to talk." On the other hand, I was already drunk, and wasn't a heroin hangover preferable to the alcohol kind any day of the week? Pink boxer shorts with black dots peeked from beneath her short skirt. Okay, if Jane thought it was okay, then it was okay. Truly it was no big deal.

She brushed powder from the corner of my mouth, then gazed into the mirror. "Yesterday Julie and Tim were like, 'What's going on between you two?' Meaning you and me. And I was like, 'Why is everyone obsessed with our business? Can't we have one second of privacy?'" She snapped the compact shut and dropped it in her purse. "C'mon. I'll walk you home."

When we reached the heroin shopping market, Jane grabbed my arm. "Here's a cigarette," she said, as though handing me a cyanide pill before sending me behind enemy lines. There are these events lying in the future, poisonous bulbs in frozen soil. Days pass and your body moves toward them, the soil relaxes and the bulbs stir and ascend, pushing up through the warm ground to begin their deadly unfurling. She lit my cigarette, scanning the street. "They always think I'm a cop," she said. "I'll wait over there."

Later that night we sat sprawled on the sidewalk, leaning against the chain-link fence of a playground, snorting dope from Jane's MetroCard with a dollar bill and vomiting companionably, debris from her purse scattered around us. At some point I ran across to the bodega for two quarts of Bud. We covered a variety of topics, our conversation roamed among the planets and stars and our voices rang in the street as the time-lapse moon soared and the untouched bottles of beer sat brownly beside us. For weeks afterward I'd see the beers in Jane's refrigerator, still untouched, sealed with Saran Wrap and rubber bands. "Jane, do you ever get that thing where suddenly you're blasted into a long nauseating plunge down an icy glass chute of despair straight into the crevasse of some weird narrative con-trolling your thoughts?" I inquired, lighting a cigarette. "I don't know," Jane said, "but I feel like that wall across the street is a sonic boom against my eyeballs." We were thrown back against the fence by our own hilarity. Time flew by so quickly on the dope that each time I looked up the sky was lighter by several shades of blue. "Is the moon full?" I yelled repeatedly, though it quite clearly was, hanging first low above the housing proj-ects before us, then overhead, finally visible only when we turned our heads.

"On the radio last night some guy said he'd grown up in Nevada during the halcyon days of nuclear testing," I reported, "and he swore that when he and his brother knew there was going to be a test, they'd wait with a detached car hood and when the blast wave hit their yard they'd surf it with the hood." "That definitely happened," Jane said. "So I finally finished that Anne Sexton thing, and I decided that I'm Anne Sexton and you're Maxine Kumin." I stopped trying to make our sticks of gum line up perpendicular to a crack in the sidewalk. "You fuckhead!" I shouted. "No one even knows who Maxine Kumin is! Including me and I read the book!" I grabbed my cigarette stub from the can of Coke and took a drag. "But she's the smart one," Jane protested, laughing. "Whose poetry sucks," I said. I flicked the cigarette toward the street. It flew about an inch, bouncing off my shoe. "I want to be Anne Sexton," I said, "even though I can't believe you're making me have this stupid conversation." "Okay, we can both be Anne Sexton," Jane said, holding the Metro-Card while I tapped out some powder. "Perfect," I said, putting the dollar bill to my nose and leaning over. "But secretly you're Maxine Kumin," she said, as I sniffed up the line. My heart thrummed smoothly in my chest and I felt so delicious I slid down to rest my cheek on the burning concrete. "Oh, Jane, you're a wily one," I sighed, gazing at her long bare legs extended next to me. Birds sang in the darkness and I was vaguely aware of Jane snipping away at her bangs with nail clippers, gazing into the compact mirror balanced on her knee. Interestingly, a pair of filthy socks stood erect before me. "Can I trouble you young ladies for a cigarette?" We looked up. A bum lurched above us, toothless and, I now understood, minus shoes. "Sure, take a bunch," I said magnanimously, pushing the pack toward him and rolling on my back.

"Are you real?" asked Jane. "That depends," he replied. Jane looked at me. "En-ig-ma-tic," she mouthed as the guy stuffed our pack of cigarettes into his coat. Who cared, we had more. He extended a filthy paw down toward my face. "Bye," Jane said. "Allow me to kiss your hand before departing, dear," he offered nobly. I smiled up at him, stifling a recoil. "Oh that's okay," I responded politely. "But thanks. We're kind of busy." "Oh, you're lesbians!" he exclaimed, placing his hand over his heart. "That is SO cool! Cuz just between you girls and me—" he looked around conspiratorially, "I myself am a lesbian trapped in the body of a man." "Oh you FUCKER!" I cried, sitting up. "You assholes have everything, but you've just got to have that one last little thing, don't you?" "Yeah," said Jane. "That's the oldest creepiest line in the book and we hear it fifty times a day." "Exactly," I said, lying back down. The bum looked confused but he turned away. Jane rolled her eyes as he wandered off.

"What is my fucking life?" She slumped back against the fence. "Why don't I care about anything anymore? I used to be so young and frisky and full of hope." I pushed myself up again from the sidewalk. "Oh, Jane, you care!" I said, brushing grit from my cheek. "You crazy nut! Your problem is you care too much!"

"I guess you're right," she said, gazing mournfully at the bodega. "So, Damon came over last night. And of course he had drugs. I wanted to talk about me and him because I think there's still something there, but he just kept obsessing on Lisa, while we were lying on the bed!" The street swung before me in blue moonlight dazzle and a tropical haze bloomed from the bodega neon. "What's his fucking problem?" I shouted. According to Jane,weren't she and Damon *just friends* now, since supposedly she was *so totally over his shit*?

Jane pulled out her lipstick, continuing to talk as she applied it. "And I was like, 'Why do I have to listen to this shit about a girl who, actually, I myself used to have a crush on?'" She capped the lipstick and pulled a container of powdered blush from her purse. "I got kind of nauseous before he left," she continued, "so he was like, 'Well, let me just sit with you on the bed for a minute to make sure you're okay.' And then he started touching me."

"Ruh-roh!" I yelped, like the dog I was. A cartoon knife stabbed rhythmically into my thorax. Must she feed on the hearts of everyone in town? "So he's touching me," she said, "and of course it feels fantastic, so I'm like, 'Why don't you sleep over and we can talk?' And he says, 'I have to go.'"

"Mmm," I nodded thoughtfully. "Hmm." They were both complete idiots and parenthetically they could go fuck themselves in a hall of motherfucking mirrors. "In *Civilization and Its Discotheques* Freud says that life and love as we know it are just too hard," I offered by way of fake commiseration. "That discovery alone makes him one of our world's greatest minds," Jane said, unwrapping a stick of gum. "Spotlight back on me: Damon's like 'I have to go,' and I just screamed at him, 'You make me come and now you just want to fucking *leave*?'"

At Jane's use of the word "come," I flushed. Unironic talk with her of sex that she'd actually had always mortified me. For some reason whenever I had a crush on someone it seemed that surely they must kiss and have sex in another language, some alien dimension whose superior and decorous inhabitants looked down bemused upon the odd grapplings of the humans, their peculiar and laughable Makings of the Love. "I mean, why would he do that?" Jane insisted. I worried she could read my mind as I pictured her coming at the touch of the behemoth Damon, or, as I enjoyed referring to him in my mind, Daemon; I tried to imagine what Jane would be like, coming, and for a moment

I saw her face, eyes closed, hand gripping the back of my neck, before I was suddenly displaced and erased by Daemon, whose image I immediately smashed beneath a cinder block of revulsion. Sex on heroin was bewitching and absurd, you were swoony with everything, but you couldn't come, at least in my experience. I'd gone home with a stranger one night high on dope and cocaine, taken off my clothes and joined him in the shower, stunning him and myself with my lack of inhibition. I felt like a porn star and it was great, we had sex all over his apartment, not really coming but exclaiming repeatedly to one another in astonishment, "Oh my god, call me crazy but I love you so much!"

As blood dripped down my torso from my lacerated heart, I felt a sudden and inexplicable tenderness toward Jane for confiding in me. "Am I so unlovable?" she said. Stars and planets flared across the cobalt sky. I leaned toward her, bracing myself with a hand on the sidewalk to keep from falling into her lap. "Jane, listen," I said. "Uh-oh," she yelled.

"Don't worry," I said. "It's totally okay." I lit a cigarette. "I just want to say you've been totally great to put up with me bugging you. And to still stay my friend." "I know, but it's not the stalking I mind so much." She fumbled around in her purse. "I wish we had some cocaine. It's just I've been worried about you. Where's the other pack of cigarettes?" She found them, ripped off the cellophane, lit one up. "I was telling Vickie Highline how I feel helpless, like you're spinning out of control, and, I don't know, maybe we should take a break or something. Vickie's worried you might pull me down into the quicksand with you." She turned her head and threw up on the sidewalk, being at this point too lazy even to stand and walk the two feet to the curb next to a parking meter where we'd been throwing up all night.

"You were talking about me to Vickie Highline?" I said, lighting a cigarette while our shadows ran over the curb into the street. "Those shadows are making me question reality," I commented. "You've got two cigarettes burning," Jane replied, picking up the dollar bill. I looked down at the Coke can. Of course it was true. I stabbed one cigarette out on the pile of butts next to me. Was I nothing but need? "You were talking about me to Vickie?" I said again.

"Yeah, sort of, and she said the best way to help you would be—" Jane leaned over and snorted a line, "—would be—" she did the other one, "—to detach with love." She sat up and shook her head. "Whoa. Jesus." A cold flame of blue dread ignited in my chest. "Oh sure," I said. "I totally understand. Definitely. Detach with love. Everyone says that's all you can do. It's what I would say, if I were your friend."

I came to on a misty street, cigarette burning down between my fingers. I didn't know where I was, though buildings tilting around me felt familiar. I was going home or trying to visit someone. My heart pounded and incoherent symptoms agitated like birds, rodents, insects in my chest. Cars hydroplaned slowly behind me on the slippery asphalt. Where the fuck was I? I was standing on the front steps of a brownstone. I looked down at my hands. Cigarette in one, burned down to the filter, keys in the other, one of them already fitted in a lock, which wouldn't turn. Whose house was this?

A siren started up, I blacked out again, and then I was reeling alone down a black street, smiling at a skinny type walking past. Carnation petals and garbage floated on a slick in the gutter. The yellow haze of streetlights and green neon kept getting mixed up in my head with some kind of choir, again and again I knocked on the wrong door. *Sorry.* I intended to purchase a sponge. Vapors leaked up from the sewer grates. Signal lights swam in, green and red fishies winking in the murk. For some reason it felt okay to be walking down a sidewalk that dipped and slanted up, a sidewalk that undulated and sang on its way to nowhere, on my invisible legs, a ghost detached from some distant scene of slaughter and licking. *This is great,* I thought. *My difficulties are a thing of the past.* The ATM was many, many things: aquarium, decontamination chamber in a nuclear plant, annex to the asylum waiting room a few blocks north. Fluorescent yellow light slid down the plate-glass windows and reverberated from the tile. People drifted by outside on the sidewalk, merry clown fish and surly predators whose cold white eyes I prayed wouldn't swivel to lock on me. The screens throbbed, blue diagnostic tools. If I received the machine's approval it would spit out bills, a medic dispensing chemicals to neutralize my mistakes. In the corner a tangle of rags and human limbs stirred and mumbled. Rivulets of piss from beneath the gray heap ran diagonally across the room to the opposite corner. The floor-to-ceiling windows, the citizenry in dark raincoats withdrawing currency, glancing at the rags, stepping over the piss, walking away. Oily yellow light greasing the tiles.

My balance was thirty dollars. I took it all. Swift calculations revealed that, with the cash in my pocket, I could buy three bags of dope and still have eleven dollars to survive on until my check showed up sometime next week. It'd be totally great—I'd sup sparely on noodles and salt or maybe do a fast—a Master Cleanse! Lemons and maple syrup—pennies a day. I'd smoke with restraint, do free stuff like museums and libraries—god, how excellent, I'd be like a camping monk, or a young Indian brave tracking his lost pony through a landscape of box canyons booby-trapped with the barbs of venomous populations, subsisting only on a twig and sips of water from creeks threading silverly across the mesas as the changing seasons offered fresh and increasingly refined scourges of solitude and doubt, the intrepid young seeker traversing these infernal domains immune in his loincloth, for his quest was propelled by ecstatic devotion to his best friend and spirit guide, the dappled pony, Little Paint.

Exiting the ATM, I ran into an emaciated girl in the vestibule, a paper cup in her hand. She had on disintegrating tennis shoes with pointy toes and a shabby overcoat swallowed up her tiny frame, though the damp night was warm. She looked like a gnarled broom, a broom carved as an objet d'art by tribal artisans famed for investing even mundane household tools with the magic of the spirit world, paying homage and giving thanks, in this case to the sinister yet somewhat petty god of sweeping. She was a stick with a little misshapen face carved out beneath the hair, everything about her was pointy and sharp: tennis shoes and nose, teeth that seemed filed, her pinched mouth coming to a point. She was young but furrows radiated from her lips. All the things she'd never expressed had escaped from between her sealed lips and slithered off, their invisible corrosive bodies etching escape trails into her upper lip. The lines around her mouth formed a record of expulsions and exile and punishments for speaking. I was able to discern this because I was in the midst of an epiphany and my clarity of vision extended to all beings.

Walking to the bank, I'd realized that, actually, it was good I'd been drinking and doing drugs for most of my adult life—I mean, off and on. I was crazy to beat myself up about it, because this was the spiritual task god had set before me and I had admirably risen to the challenge. But now it was April, the month I was born, ideal for a symbolic rebirth at the close of a job well done. To kick things off I planned to buy the distinctive long-handled sponge I'd dreamed of for months but instantly forgot when I left the apartment, a peerless implement designed to reach into glasses exactly like those cluttering my kitchen. I didn't have the sponge because I only thought of it when trying to jam my fist far enough into a tumbler to remove cigarette filters cemented to the bottom. As soon as I stepped away from the glasses of soapy water lined up next to the sink, where they would remain for days, "soaking," all memory of the sponge was erased until I either approached the dishes again, spotted an ergonomically handled scrubber next to someone's sparkling sink, or stumbled across one at the A&P when I only had enough money for cigarettes and cat food.

I myself was a tremendous filter for toxins, a giant toxic sponge, and, like Job, I had learned many valuable lessons. But the time had come to relinquish my poison-absorption duties to a professional, the long-handled sponge. I would make my pilgrimage tomorrow to the store and upon returning home I would place the new device behind the sink, perhaps in a ceremonial vessel of some kind to mark the passing of the torch, the renewal of my birthday vows.

No, you know what? I was going to buy the sponge tonight. The A&P was open twenty-four hours. No more putting things off. When I woke I'd be greeted by the sponge and a day entirely free of commercial transactions. I didn't want to taint my purification before it even got off the ground with the capitalistic exchange of filthy lucre. Tomorrow it was going to be a snap to quit. In fact, with sponge in hand it would be virtually impossible not to quit. Before now, quitting would have been irresponsible, indeed sacrilegious, and a shirking of my god-prescribed duty to investigate and report from the unlit corners of life. Actually it was noble of me to have continued abusing drugs and alcohol until this moment, and I felt the reverent melancholy of farewell as I contemplated abusing my final bags of dope tonight in the presence of the sacred revivifying sponge.

"Hi," I said to the girl with the cup. "Here." I held out a five-dollar bill. "Wow, thanks." She had a row of crusty sores along her lower lip. "No problem," I replied, weav-

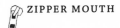 **ZIPPER MOUTH**

ing a little as I stood before her. "I know what it's like to be a girl." The door buzzed and we both stepped back as a woman blew past in stiletto heels. I rolled my eyes. "God, you must be so strong," I observed. "I try to give money to girls because I think it's harder for us than anyone. Especially on the street. Not to be all presumptuous, like I have any idea what it's like for you."

"Oh it's totally fine." She smiled and a ghost, her double, stepped out from her side. Together they opened their mouths, speaking in the electronic Voice of Evil favored by so many demons. "I was a nurse in El Paso," they confided.

"Whoa! Outstanding!" I yelled, staggering back. "Wait—what?" I braced myself against the wall.

"Worse things have happened," repeated the girl.

"Oh, whew!" I had no idea what she meant, but that was cool. I closed one eye and the evil twin vanished. "Hey," I whispered, leaning in. "I just want you to know that this society—" The buzzer sounded and I lost my train of thought. As change jingled into her cup, she glanced past my shoulder. I stepped back. "Don't listen to me, you crazy nut!" I said humorously. "You've got a job to do!" I nodded toward some guy inserting his card in the slot. "And I'm not helping! Look, I'm leaving."

"No, it's totally okay," she said as the door buzzed and the guy passed between us. "Okay, well, here I go!" I said. "Great talking to you and have an awesome night."

I lurched away but turned when the inner door behind me opened on the line at the ATM. "I'm sorry this society's so mean and full of hate," I informed everyone loudly, craftily pretending to address the girl. "Maybe a few pennies will trickle down from some marketing exec's embezzling spree"—was I shouting?—"so that you can buy a tiny doughnut." In deference to the girl I decided against slamming the door behind me. On the sidewalk I brushed against a man cruising up in his raincoat, probably a stockbroker. "Fuck you," I said. I felt happy.

There are multiple copies of my mother, and every time I turn my head one of them flits past the edge of my vision. For my wedding in the Future, she prepared a Hope Chest, some kind of old-school tradition. She purchased a cedar box upholstered on the outside with fake leopard skin and put secret things inside. The Hope Chest has a lock, and I'm not supposed to know what's inside until I open it, I guess on my wedding day. Except I know that in reality the Hope Chest contains the body of my father's secretary. I know this because there are drops of blood in the hall and I can hear Mom and Dad whispering about something in their room down the hall. Plus I have a brain tumor, I'm pretty sure. At midnight I glide expertly through the sleeping house and out the front door in utter silence before sprinting down the block to my friend Doreen's.

"Sit down, honey," Doreen's mother says before disappearing into the kitchen. The dad wanders around while she makes the call, her low voice behind the wall demanding, "What's going on over there? This child's staying here until we straighten things out." Or so I imagine. Five minutes later she returns to communicate silently, via Adult Eye Contact, with her husband, and within minutes we're floating in their car down the dark street toward my house. Riding to school the next day in this same vehicle Doreen and I make *Yikes!* faces at one another in the backseat while her mother, after barely acknowledging me, stares rigidly ahead in silence. Does Doreen know? My corpuscles flash-frozen into crystals of ice, I can barely move my jaw when it comes time to say, "Thanks for the ride, Mrs. Rossman!"

When I opened the Hope Chest I actually felt kind of excited. I was probably twenty or so when I finally turned the key in my chest. My mother was either teary with sentimentality or peculiarly indifferent, I seem to recall both. Though maybe she was just embarrassed and sad. Possibly I'd openly ridiculed it as a teenager, unwittingly humiliated her into abandoning the project; another dream dies. Two dreams, actually, for fundamentally I was in love with the idea of my mother having a dream, any fantasy that had thrilled her as a child when she thought of it coming true in the future. Lining the inner floor of the chest about a half inch deep were a few embroidered pillowcases. Otherwise it was empty.

September light shattered against the cars. The usual buzzing in my head and sensation of skidding toward psychosis had begun. I didn't care. I am happy today, I reflected, flaming along, torched by the sun. Sunlight showered down onto hubcaps, bike rims, chain-link fencing, aluminum cans. How best to use the gleaming day? As always the first item on the agenda was to call in sick to work. People holding paper cups of coffee, heads teeming with goals and five-year plans, strode by while store owners hosed down their little scraps of sidewalk, each head illuminated by a medieval gold corona. How was it that I wasn't scrubbing for neurosurgery as per my blueprints for the future back in sixth grade? How was it that I didn't care? The world ablaze around me, a gift. I feel splendid, gliding through the singing luminosity of the day. I need to detox and detox begins at home. Laundry.

As a rule I was constitutionally incapable of dealing with the laundry in its various stages, i.e., getting it off the floor when dirty and into Hefty bags, where it rested for several days, then across the street to the laundromat. Once freshly washed the clothes would make their perilous journey back across the avenue to be dumped from the Hefty bag onto the bed, but for the clothing, making it to safety in the closet or dresser was like escaping from prison in a murderous totalitarian regime and then, once outside the prison walls, trekking for weeks across a forbidding and treacherous landscape, chased, starving, shot at and frostbitten, before finally staggering up to the sea on the bloody stumps of your former feet to hang with the rat swarms beneath a wharf until such day as a small freighter chugged into view and you were smuggled into its airless hold to sail the open seas for weeks before being hurled into the turbulent churn by a storm of freakish intensity, there to bob shivering until the US Coast Guard plucked you up and hustled you off to prison, where the INS kept you for years before denying your petition for asylum, ultimately returning you to your murderous regime to be drawn and quartered, but not until you'd watched your entire family be chopped into bits. This is how my laundry felt, especially when struggling to resist the brutal hope which came with making it safely back from the laundromat to the bed. The clothing knew full well not to allow itself the yearning delusion that this time things would work out, because, in the first place, the bed itself, like the stormy sea, was in an uproar, and many items of apparel simply disappeared in the tangle of books and blankets, never to be recovered. If I managed to fold the laundry there remained the issue of sorting it, after several days at the earliest, into stacks. Once sorted, the stacks lingered near the drawers only inches away, so near yet so far, my underwear and socks drifting gradually toward the wall, there to topple slowly as I kicked the neat piles in my sleep, the increasingly rumpled clothes being now susceptible to layers of black cat hair, for Steve and Cherry loved the soft pants and shirts slipping helplessly to the floor between mattress and footboard to mingle with dust balls and the leftover B-list clothes not deemed important enough to launder in the first round.

Yet always the freshly washed clothes awakened from this dream to find themselves hangdog and wilted, though never worn, by the filth of the floor and the weighty vibe of my oppressive nights. So usually I ended up rewashing after approximately one month the so-called clean items along with the newly soiled ones, by now there being no discernible difference except to a forensic pathologist, which clearly I am not, though I admit it has always been a dream of mine, but what hasn't, but my point is that these repeated extra washings, which rarely resulted in wearing, incurred, if you calculated it in terms of yearly output, untold extra financial expense and who knows what social cost due to unsightly outfits thrown together in desperation, so that what started out as a happy and hopeful occasion—the impulse to pull myself up from the muck of paralysis to cleanse and renew myself at the Lourdes of the Laundromat—somehow managed to add yet more poundage to the anvil of demoralization dragging me further each day into a primal bubbling stew of self-disgust that once had been a shallow fount of pristine warm springwaters in which I gurgled, a naked cherub laughing and waving my fists, waiting to be kissed by the elephants, giraffes, and wildebeests that came to the oasis where I lay because they wanted to play with me and help—the elephant, so emotional and washing me gently in warm mists from her trunk; the giraffe, also gentle plus tenderly putting her lips to mine with leaves from the forest canopy; the wildebeest, she says to me, "Do not wander too far from your herd, I saw on the Discovery Channel what happens when weaker animals wander too far from the herd." She nuzzled me, in fact they all nuzzled me, and I wish I were back with them still. They were psychic and smart and now that I am composed entirely of sin like a black wax voodoo doll, I miss my playmates. I wish not to be human, we're the lowest form of life, we think big thoughts but there's nothing to think, good decisions bad decisions it's all the same, like the song the animals sing:

Fuck. Up. The people!
You meet 'em wherever you go . . .
Moosies, use your antlers!
Humans cause us so much woe . . .

A hoof in the forehead!
Stampede 'em wherever you go . . .
Peck them until dead!
Scorched Earth is all they know . . .

Meercats! Maul the people!
You're too sweet, you gotta say No.
Because extincting the people
Is now our only hope!

The other evening I found myself in a park by the river, a sad park at the far end of the bombed-out zone of the city, a slick of silver moonlight shining on the river, crack vials glittering on the asphalt running track. I was alone except for homeless people passed out or huddled on benches. It was like being in the woods, invisible menace all around. Knife blades twinkled among the leaves and shadows flitted across the black grass scarred with bald patches like a radiation victim's scalp. A landscape like this, toxic water, industrial waste vats along the shore, smokestacks inside a chemical sky, used to fill me with erotic pain and I would think about death and being in love. Now I don't have heavy emotions though within the circuitry of bridge spans and chain-link fencing my body is a soft machine; it will decay and disappear.

She got me in the crosswalk at Seventh and B when I had the dealer in my crosshairs, or rather the dealer's proxy, some guy in a green plastic poncho pretending to fuss over the vegetable stand in front of the market where he worked for pennies a day. Happy to help supplement his income, I headed across the street. Everything was black. My black jacket, black park behind me, asphalt black, buildings black, even the streetlights were ringed in black. It was cold. I couldn't think so I didn't about all the times I'd crossed this intersection alone at night in the last seven years, seven years since I'd moved to the city, when I was afraid to go east of A, since the night I waited in a bar while Tony copped and returned to lay a white line out on the table and I thought, What the hell. It was okay, because at the time I didn't drink. You couldn't go through life without trying heroin, if you were to fully live you had to do it, like many kinds of sex. Plus, the sophistication of doing dope right out in public! No one even glanced our way. Tonight no one was out. I didn't care, I wasn't scared. To work through my hangover I'd gotten drunk at *In Cold Type* with my psycho boss Andy and the rest of his coked-up fun-loving staff and somehow I ended up getting out of a cab by the river and now I was back over here at Seventh and B, and fine. Fine with me. The guy glowed greenly above his vegetables. Even the bar on the corner seemed empty, no bouncer, no drunken hipsters spilling outside. A hooded figure in a black coat scurried past me in the crosswalk then pulled up short.

"Hi!" she said brightly behind me. I turned and peered. A grinning bed of nails glinted out at me from beneath a druid hood. The homeless girl from the ATM. My stomach sank. A few strands of broom hair escaped the hood, hissing orange. I was too drunk to defend myself. "Oh, hey!" I said. "What's going on?" she asked, super friendly. I should have said I was on my way to a friend's. Something in my head told me to lie; if I was sober I'd have lied but the need for drugs, of course she would know where to get them . . . was it just yesterday I'd promised myself I'd never drink again, and that when I did, I'd have enough sense to recognize trouble and go home alone immediately. Yesterday morning I'd said this to myself, all this flashed through my head in the intersection and I said, "I was going to try and cop from that guy." "Okay," she said, "let me do it. How many do you want?" "Four," I replied. I didn't even remember getting money. "Okay," she said. "Wait here." I gave her the cash and turned to look interestedly at a tree in the park. Two seconds later she was back. "Not tonight. But I know where we can get it." "Okay," I said. Then, thinking there was some sort of gentleman's agreement involved here, I offered, "I'll buy me three bags and you a bag." "You don't have to do that," she protested sweetly. "No, no, I insist," I said. It was like we were on a date. We walked a while. I was tired. She disappeared around a corner with my money. Fine, I thought, rip me off. At least I'll be rid of you. I desperately wanted her to disappear and just as desperately I wanted her to return with drugs. A wind blew up the deserted street, sucking bits of trash into the air, rattling the corrugated doors on the storefronts. It was like postwar Prague. It was like Prague now, for all I knew. A car alarm went off, signaling the end of the world. I'm calm, I thought, I'm really calm. The girl reappeared, a shadow peeling itself from the wall. She had dope. With the certainty of drugs, I felt a surge of elation and goodwill. We'd go home and have some laughs. Plus, she was homeless; surely I could offer her a break from this freezing weather? Also, she hadn't handed over the bags yet and I couldn't figure out a polite way to ask her for my drugs and walk away. I didn't want her to think I was just using her, which I totally was. Climbing the stairs to my place, I prayed my neighbors wouldn't see us.

I snorted a line. Right away I knew it was heroin,

not fentanyl or whatever that synthetic shit was, the surgical anesthetic. Benevolence rushed through me. "What can I get you?" I said. "Let me make you some tea." "I don't want anything," she replied, rummaging in her stuff. She carried a huge plastic bag and inside that was a paper shopping bag filled with smaller plastic bags, bag after bag, crammed with what looked like random scraps of paper. She pulled out a quart of milk and put it in my fridge when I directed her toward the microscopic extra room where it lived with the litter box to save space in my kitchen. It was like watching a deranged Mary Poppins. Now that I had my dope I wanted her out, of course, but she kept unpacking.

She was so smooth I almost missed it when she shot up. I bent over the plate with my rolled-up dollar bill and sniffed. When I raised my head, she had a tiny syringe hanging from her forearm. It startled me. I'd forgotten that people still shoot up. "You don't mind, do you?" she asked, jacking blood back and forth in the tube. "God, no!" I laughed suavely. On the table had appeared a strip of sealed syringes, cotton swabs, a wee bottle of alcohol, a bottle cap filled with fluid, and next to that a lemon. She toyed with her blood, pushing the plunger in and out but never all the way in, talking at the same time, barely paying attention to the procedure with her arm. Though she herself was so sickly, her arms looked strong, the veins ropy. "You know what?" I exclaimed.

"Here you are, my guest, and I don't even know your name." She drove the blood from the syringe back into her vein and I exhaled with relief.

"My name's Tammy," she said, pulling the needle from her arm and placing an orange cap over the tip. "That was so cool of you to give me five bucks that one night at the cash machine."

"Oh, no problem," I lied. "I can afford it because I'm working right now. What's that lemon for?"

"It dissolves the crack back into pure coke," she replied, stowing the syringe in her pocket. "I'm doing speedballs."

"Oh, sure." I nodded. We sat there. Her outline softened as the drugs hit, her bones and skin deflated. I felt pretty boneless myself, though not quite high enough to paralyze the hamsters of unease running on their miniature treadmills in my stomach. I tried to think of some fun conversational gambits. "So, Tammy," I said. "What are we gonna do with you, ya kook? How we gonna get you off the streets?" Her eyes roved dully around my kitchen for a moment. Abruptly she brightened. "Hey!" she said. "All right! So you do have at least a little taste." I followed her gaze, which had zeroed in on my kitchen shelf and the dominant, well actually the only, food item on the premises, a box of Trix, featuring blue pellets. "Oh, right!" I enthused. "I really love cold cereal!"

The evening in Tammy's company stretched before me, the eight or nine hundred hours until dawn. She showed no signs of going anywhere. How would I escape? Hastily, I began talking about my new girlfriend, Jane, making it up as I went along, how she worked the overnight at a restaurant and would head over here to spend the night when she got off work at four. "We're in that weird phase where we can't get enough of each other, and just totally don't want to see other people," I hinted. "Great," said Tammy absently. "I'd love to meet your girlfriend." She was looking past me at the window when suddenly her eyes narrowed in suspicion. "What's wrong?" I said, turning. The Venetian blind behind me was open just enough to reveal a brick wall. "That's just a window well, Tammy. What's wrong?" "King's obsessed with spying on me," she said. "Well, you don't have to worry about anything out there," I laughed. "There's no fire escape or anything. No one can get back there." She pulled a compact from one of her bags, snapped it open, and twisted in the chair so that her back faced me. She held the compact out in front of her brow. "You'd be surprised," she said, tilting the mirror at various angles to search for something over her shoulder. I stood up. "Here, let's shut the blinds."

When I turned back to the table, Tammy had materialized in the cat box/refrigerator room facing the street. She crouched slightly, scanning the night through a slat in the blinds while simultaneously holding the compact up to reflect the room behind her. "What's shakin' over there, Tammy?" I called out jovially. Clearly, she was insane. It was that fucking speedball. Cocaine is an evil drug. I walked into the cat litter room. "Tammy?" I said gently. She didn't turn around. The compact was so close to her face that she couldn't possibly have seen anything reflected but her eye. "Sometimes," she informed herself darkly, as though privately reviewing the facts in order to assess the threat level, "King hires people to invite me into their apartments so he can watch me from a rooftop across the street." A little elevator dropped from my esophagus to my pelvis, spewing self-loathing and exasperation as it fell. This situation, managing the mentally ill, was utterly familiar, and I had only myself to blame. I recalled visiting Tony right after he'd done a speedball to find him standing in one place in his living room, sweating and shifting from foot to foot. Out of the blue he sank to his knees then stretched out full length to peer beneath the front door on his stomach, still wearing his suit from his programming job on Wall Street. There was nothing to see because the door extended all the way to the floor; there wasn't a crack or anything. "I think there might be cops out there," he said. I opened the door. "Tony, there are no cops. Sit down and relax. I'll watch for the cops." He looked nervous but stood up and moved to the couch.

After a moment he said, "I know this sounds crazy, but I think there's a rat sitting on the doorknob."

There was no way I could reason with Tammy now; I couldn't imagine how I'd get her out of the apartment and down the stairs without calling the cops and waking the neighbors. It occurred to me that she could kill me or something, but on the other hand, I was too high to panic. Really, it seemed okay.

"Well, this is great," I said. "You can sleep on the futon." I slid a clean if slightly befurred pillowcase from beneath Cherry on the bed, shifted her onto a fluffy sweater, and repaired to the living room to make a lovely bed with fresh orange sheets for Tammy, who meanwhile had shifted surveillance operations to the front door, where she stood frozen with one eyeball glued to the peephole, the other mashed up against her mirror. "Everything okay?" I sang. She raised the compact like a periscope above her head, the mirror glinting in my direction. "It's all good," she breathed dramatically, maintaining focus. I snorted about four more lines. They hit and I was feeling magnificent, a wise love machine. I recalled another occasion when the heroin shopping market around the corner had closed right before I could cop, and I'd invited one of the hipster guys in line to come to my apartment to wait with me for five minutes until it reopened. He said he was a filmmaker who was *going straight into rehab the second I fin-*

ish this shoot in France. I'd gone to pee and left a lot of cash sitting on the table in front of him. When I came back, he hadn't touched it. Really, junkies you bring in off the street can be quite nice.

I decided to make some phone calls while Tammy drifted about. I said a lot of shit on the phone. My friend was feeling angry and hopeless. I gave her a long lecture about right and wrong, drugs having clarified for me the issues of good versus evil, getting up periodically to check on Tammy, who returned again and again to the peephole as though she were buried underground, trying to get a glimpse of life up above. After a while I quit worrying. I told my friend I loved her. I was on the phone a long time. When I hung up, I went looking for my guest and found her nodding off on the toilet, torso slumped between her knees, her hair, the color of B vitamins in piss, sweeping the floor.

"Come on, darling," I said. Slowly her head lifted. I took her hand. "Let's go. You gotta go to bed. You're nodded out."

"That's just because I'm sitting down," she said. "I see your point," I said, "but come on, I'll get you a T-shirt and boxers and you'll climb into nice clean sheets and go to sleep. Okay?"

"Okay," she said, pulling up her pants, suddenly docile. "Can I take a shower first?" "Nope," I said cheerily. "You'll nod off and fall down."

"Okay," she said. She shuffled into the kitchen. I got her the boxers and T-shirt. "Now come on," I said again firmly, resisting the urge to yank her arm. "Change your clothes and get in bed. It's all clean." I was desperate to get her to sleep so the night would be over and it would be morning and she'd be out of my fucking house. When I drunkenly gave her five dollars at the ATM that night, whatever night that was, did I ever dream she'd end up sleeping in my house?

Tammy headed for the living room with her clothes. Abruptly, she stopped, swaying, then turned around and trundled back to the bathroom. "I gotta take a shower," she mumbled. I sighed. God fucking *dammit*. But I should lighten up, right? She was homeless. A shower would feel great. "Okay," I said, "here's a towel." I gave her my last clean towel. "You can just hang your clothes on that bar." "No," she said, "I want to wash them in the shower." "Oh," I said. "Of course. Excellent! But how will they dry?" "I'll put them on the radiator," she replied. I thought of David Lynch's *Eraserhead*, the lady inside the radiator singing that beautiful song "In Heaven Everything Is Fine." I gave up. Tammy's motherfucking clothes would never be dry by morning but whatever. I couldn't think. While she showered I lit a cigarette and roamed the apartment, waiting to hear the crack of skull against porcelain. Her shower went on and on. I paced, I smoked, I snorted, I leafed through *Living Without a Goal*. Inspired, I opened up my journal and jotted down some thoughtful musings. I changed channels on TV to *Devil Dog: The Hound of Hell*, starring Yvette Mimieux and Richard Crenna. It was pretty good.

In detox there was one videotape available for our amusement and every night at 8 p.m. the nurse passed around snack trays loaded with repulsive things like Jell-O and off-brand cookies, the same stuff bodegas stock for junkies. While the fur flew in the so-called lounge area of detox, which was basically a grade-school cafeteria, as the girls scrambled for their pink drinks with foil seals and accused each other of snack thievery and double-crossing, these young girls who for the most part had three or four children of their own, the nurse turned on the video, which every night turned out to be *Jurassic Park*. Sometimes, having exhausted my reading supply, I'd slouch into a plastic orange chair to watch, chain-smoking and eating my goddamn junkie cookie, and once when Laura Dern chanced upon a triceratops, a girl shouted, "Holy shit. Look at that. That shit's for real! Where'd he find that?" Another girl said, "That's not real, you asshole, dinosaurs are extinct."

"You can't make up shit like that!"

"They can do anything with special effects, goddammit!"

"Yeah," said another girl. "There's no dinosaurs any-more. You have brain death from heron. Don't let the nurse hear, she'll think you're high." In detox heroin became heron, the accent equal on both syllables. I felt absurdly proper calling it heroin but everyone was very nice to me and I liked our conversations on the porch, especially with Marion. At thirty-four she had no front teeth and nine children, whom she talked of taking to the zoo in a line like baby ducks. I wanted to do something to make her life be okay. I had this tiny slit of window into my fellow detoxers' lives and their acquiescence to their non-condom-wearing boyfriends and it crushed me with despair, though I should talk, I thought. I myself had terminated the occasional preg-nancy back in the day, being too shy in my early twen-ties—even after abortion number one—to tell the guy, who happened to be my boyfriend, to put one on, or to explain that I myself hadn't done much in the way of prevention. And what about that time in my first rehab, age twenty-eight, when I'd given a blow job to the ex-con from Detroit? He'd used needles his whole life, he'd been in prison. The first time he looked at me I knew he hated women, his eyes locked on me with such brutal coldness, truly I was looking into the barrels of a shot-gun. I never forgot that sensation, yet a couple of days later I found myself on my knees before him, and I let him come in my mouth and then I swallowed, panicking about AIDS, but I didn't want to hurt his feelings by spitting it out. After that every man in the rehab treated me with utter contempt.

Now every time Yvette Mimieux smoked I smoked with her. At one point I got up and wandered to a window. The water continued in the bathroom, but otherwise Tammy made no sound. Yvette emerged with the dog from the bedroom, smoking, and wandered toward the wet bar in her sunken living room to mix a highball. This movie was really quite enjoyable, I reflected, trying to decide whether to light a cigarette or snort another line or both, and if both, in what order. A bleak strand of Christmas lights winked in an apartment window across the street. I decided to vacuum, then overruled my decision.

Finally, the water stopped. I lit a cigarette, then another. I washed a couple of dishes. After about twenty more minutes, Tammy emerged from the bathroom, dressed in the underwear I'd given her. "Hey, dude!" I shouted. "Do you feel just fabulous now, or what?" I wondered if a vengeful god tuned into people's apartments at random like we tune into TV, just to see if plots for which he's set the groundwork, proclivities he's installed on your brain's hard drive, are now playing themselves out in interesting ways, producing painful yet amusing results. "Now you can go to bed, Tammy," I said. "You'll be all relaxed from the shower."

I carried her ragged wet leggings and filthy blouse to the radiator in the living room. "We'll just put these here, and they'll be fresh in the morning." I turned around. Tammy was still in the kitchen, holding onto the sink, knees bent, head collapsed onto her chest. "Whew!" I said empathetically. "God, I have to go to bed, too. Jane'll be here any minute and I'm totally exhausted." This Jane charade wasn't doing me any good, but I'd use it to kick Tammy out first thing in the morning. Gingerly I touched her shoulder. "Here we go," I said. "We're going to bed!" She clutched the sink, swaying, then raised her head. "Okay," she said. "Just let me get ready."

She opened my cupboard and pulled out my lotion and comb. "I'd like to stay awake and meet your girlfriend," she said, rubbing moisturizer on her arms and face. "Well, who knows when she'll really get here," I said. "Sometimes she has a few drinks after work. But we'll wake up when she comes." Tammy tried to pull my comb through her hair. It went about a sixteenth of an inch before tangling with a knot. "You look great," I said. "Listen, I'm gonna go ahead and lie down." I walked into the bedroom, Tammy bent over her bags.

"What're you doing?" I said, watching her through the door. "Do you have a bowl?" she asked.

"What do you need a bowl for?"

 ZIPPER MOUTH

"I'm going to make instant pudding," she said, pulling a package from her bags. I found her a bowl and retired to my bed, rudely turning out the kitchen light as I went. She didn't seem to notice, stirring busily in the light coming from the street. Was there no such thing as taking a hint? "Do you want some?" she called. I fought a wave of nausea. "Oh, that's okay," I said. "You go ahead. I'm on the bed now. I'm really exhausted."

"I love instant pudding," Tammy said. "It's so smooth." She wandered in through the beads hanging from my doorframe and sat on the bed with her bowl. "What's on TV?" she asked, spooning pudding into her mouth. "Tammy," I said, on the verge of tears, "you gotta go to bed. I really need to be alone for a few minutes before Jane gets here." She jumped up. "Oh, my god, of course!" she cried. "No problem. I like it when people are honest." She passed back through the curtain into the kitchen, oblivious to the tiny ripping sound when her hair snagged on a bead.

"When you need your space," she called, "you need your space. It's good when you say so. I don't want you to be mad or resentful in secret because I don't want to fuck up this friendship. Right?" She drifted back into the bedroom, still holding the bowl. "You don't want to fuck up this special friendship, right?" She held out a spoonful of a viscous brown substance. "Do you want some pudding?" "Nah, maybe later," I replied. "Okay," she said. "I'm going to bed." She disappeared into the living room. I could hear her doing things—chatting to me, herself, rustling around in her bags. I stared at the orange tuft she'd left on the strand of beads.

We'd been uptown at an art thing with friends, where Jane and I repeatedly slipped off to the stairwell to do drugs and laugh. In the cab rushing downtown she sat next to me, brushing my leg with her hand. "Thank god you came out," she said loudly. "Don't make me have a feeling, Jane, goddammit!" I yelled back. Our friends in the cab laughed.

At the club Jane danced with me song after song. "You look amazing," she shouted, taking my hand. I laughed. Still holding my hand she led me through the frenzied throng toward the bathroom. As though I'd awakened to find myself at the edge of a high dive I plunged headlong once more into my crush. Behind us the bathroom door slammed, shutting us safely inside.

"I'm so in love with you," I blurted out as she peed. "I'm sorry. I try not to be, I know it's incredibly annoying if not enraging and I'm sorry, but I love you so much you're making me clinically insane." I downed my Manhattan. "Fuck!" I screamed. A manic bass line and the roar of enormous drunken lesbians pumped against the door from the club outside. Jane stood. "It's okay," she said, adjusting her skirt in front of the toilet, bare shoulder rubbing the grubby wall. Really, the bathroom seemed designed for a cat. "Things change," she said. I paused. Things change? Jane edged past me to the mirror, a complicated maneuver involving the extension of her foot between my legs where I stood facing the sink, back pressed against the wall, one hand balancing a tiny mirror with its lines of coke, the other holding a rolled dollar bill, my own reciprocal sidestep toward the toilet, Jane's cotton dress brushing my chest, our heads turned sideways, cheek to cheek, we could plummet to our deaths at any moment, me lifting the precious coke mirror above Jane's head at my chin, a fragment of her pink salamander-shaped barrette registering in the corner of my right eye, her hair flicking my cheek, her hand rifling her pocketbook for lipstick. She turned to face the mirror. "I told Vickie Highline that even though you're a mess, I'm more attracted to you than ever." She stroked the bright red tube against her lips. I did a line. She rolled her lips together and smiled at me in the mirror. "We'll talk about it." She dropped her lipstick in the purse. The crazy drums of the crazy crazy nut who called herself a DJ beat psychotically on the bathroom door, against which Jane leaned, facing me, her hand behind her on the doorknob. "Everything's fine and I love you," she said. "Now give me a kiss."

I moved toward her at the door and hesitated, not meeting her eye, then gave her a peck. She took the dollar bill and snorted a line from the mirror as I held it before my face. "Very, very fine," she said, smiling again. She pushed the mirror down and cupped my chin in her palm. Her black lashes were so thick. "This is excellent," she breathed. "Let's go find the boys."

She loved me? I stood in the middle of the club seething with lesbians entranced by disco. Tony handed me a shot and his boyfriend Danny grabbed my arm, jerking me from the corridor of linear time into the chaotic jouissance of the frothing crowd. Jane was snatched away in the current. I stood beneath the mirror ball, racing desperation in my chest. "Jane," I said to the boys. "Jane." I opened my mouth and Danny placed Ecstasy on my tongue. Lesbians surged across the dance floor, a molten wall of lava churning my body back and forth. I glimpsed Jane laughing with some girl at the bar, leaning over to shout something in her ear. "I'll buy drugs for everyone," I announced. She couldn't have heard, but Jane looked over and smiled at me, raising an eyebrow. The girl next to her looked my way. I gestured to the door. "I need air," I shouted at Jane. She nodded and smiled. I pointed again at the door. "I need air!"

I was snorting coke with a straight boy, perched on a carpeted shelf at an after-hours club. He leaned over the mirror, pushing a sugary gleam of long hair away from his face. I recalled walking, the manic golden night, stars blowing around like jacks in the sky. I was sick with longing. The dope and now coke had hit but still. The boy smiled. Life was going to be different, I couldn't think how. A life of science, devoted to research. Aesthetically, the boy was quite delicious, dark wavy hair shimmering around his shoulders, clear maple-syrup eyes, full mouth. He was gentle and beautiful and suddenly I realized that I felt no self-consciousness around him, I felt only his cotton candy and my own power. I didn't need him and this relaxed me. I smiled and told him jokes. I felt kind of bad about leading him on, but then again I didn't. Was there even such a thing as leading someone on? Well, actually I was flirting with him so I could snort his coke on the carpeted bench in the dark basement lounge, leaning back against concrete walls and smiling all come-hitherly with my sensationally opiated lips, while on the tiny square of tile that served as the dance floor drag queens with high teased wigs and skyscraper heels whirled to the mesmerizing music and held their cigarettes aloft beneath the exposed white pipes of the ceiling.

God I loved doing drugs at an after-hours club at 6 a.m. I'd been waiting for this moment since at age eleven I walked into the little head shop on the strip and bought myself an incense lamp and poster of *Easy Rider* for my ceiling. Why was this guy staying around? Was I beautiful or repulsive? Repulsive, right? But charming, no? I was lonely and I enjoyed having someone attractive to do drugs with. The boy's angelic glamour made it seem as though our union were blessed—here, let me sprinkle you with stardust. It seemed wise to remove my shirt. My bra was beautiful and my breasts, I realized, magnificent. These were heady days. I stood up and grooved my way to the dance floor, nodding my head, very Miles Davis or whoever. God, I had that natural groove thing in my veins, you were either born with it or you weren't, I had a crush on one of the drag queens and I gravitated her way. The music fractured my skull. "Jesus fuck!" I screamed. The drag queen inclined her head, smiling too. "I fucking love you!" I yelled. She extended her hand and cupped my chin, as Jane had done only moments, was it days, earlier. I spun at the center of several dancers. The boy stood next to me, turning my body while the queen I loved draped me in toilet paper, as though I were a maypole and she were spinning me in ribbons. I gave a suave thumbs-up to the DJ as I twirled. He nodded. It was evident he was impressed. The boy touched my arm, adoration pouring from those—I'm sorry—those puppy-dog eyes. "Do you want to come home with me?" I said. "I mean, not to have sex or anything. Just to hang? I have some heroin, if that's something you enjoy."

Sunlight tore into us when we exited the club. Songs of normalcy and hope poured forth from the beaks of joyous little birds, greetings to the new day. "Oh my god," I said. Young men in suits hurried through the damp morning to work, hair still wet from the shower, faces gleaming with sweat.

Rumor whispered of an early morning heroin market catering exclusively to execs, who lined up at 7 a.m. in an empty lot for their little envelopes of bliss. Had any of these guys been there? Were there hangovers, suicidal ideations behind those hearty goal-oriented demeanors?

"I'm not a slut or anything," I informed the guy. "Because we're not going to have sex. Which is not to say you would in any way subscribe to the age-old misogynistic clichés. Obviously there's no such thing as a slut." "Of course," he said. He grabbed my arm and pulled me back as I lurched into the path of an oncoming bus. "Listen," he said. "There's another after-hours club that's open from eight till noon." "Oh thank god!" I said, leaning against him for balance.

In my apartment we faced one another across a coffee table strewn with drugs, very *Scarface*, me on the couch, him on the floor. Perhaps it was 2 p.m., who could say, a Deep House tape I'd picked up on the street kept at bay the daytime noises of traffic and kids. "My favorite part in *Eraserhead*," I was explaining, "is when Eraserhead's girlfriend's just had a baby, and someone goes to him, 'How's the baby doing?' And Eraserhead says, 'They're not even sure it's a baby yet.'" I sat back and laughed for a while as the guy regarded me and nodded, smiling. I chugged some vodka. "Anyway, if someone were to ask who I identified with most in that movie, I'd say, 'The baby.'"

"You're very beautiful," said the boy. "Why are you so down on yourself?"

"Oh, no reason," I said, sprinkling catnip around for the cats so we'd all be on the same page, chemically speaking.

"I mean, couldn't you see that every drag queen in the room wanted to be you?" the guy persisted earnestly. "Now you're just talking crazy," I responded, as Cherry commenced a happy stoner dance, pirouetting coquettishly and butting her head into our legs until Steve, overstimulated, flattened her. Gallantly my gentleman caller rescued her and lifted her onto his lap. "For me," he said, stroking her ears, "gratification comes when I can clean a woman's house."

"What?" I said.

"I like to clean girls' houses."

"Are you fucking with me?" He was so gorgeous, he could be as mean to girls as he wanted.

 ZIPPER MOUTH

"No, really," he said, very composed. "It's a source of pleasure." "That's totally excellent," I said, "but, I mean, I'd feel really bad making you clean this house." I gestured around. "It's completely disgusting. Would you even clean the cat box?" He laughed. "Sure, if that's what you wanted," he said.

"No way," I said. "I could never make you clean the cat box."

"Seriously, for me, it's enjoyable to do whatever you tell me."

"I don't know," I said. "I don't think I'm a good dominatrix. I mean, I totally support it, but I'd feel bad." "Don't feel bad," he said, "because you'd be making me incredibly happy." Jesus, why didn't I just order him to put on one of my bras right now? "You know I'm a lesbian, right?" I said. "It doesn't make any difference," he said, rolling a joint.

I did a couple of lines. "Well, can we think about it?" I said. I pushed the mirror toward him. Abruptly the world started to blur and whirl. Cold sweat erupted from my pores. "Oh fuck," I gasped. "My body's rejecting me." I fell back against the couch and closed my eyes. "Maybe you'd better go," I managed, after a minute. "Okay," he responded politely. "Oh," I cried. "this is so much fun. I wanted you to stay all day!" "Are you okay?" he said, leaning across the table to place his hand on my wrist.

"Yeah, but I'm going to be amazingly sick." I forced myself to stand. I rushed him to the door, sweat pouring from my face. "Thank you for a lovely evening," I said. "I'll call you to come and clean, okay?" I opened the door. "But you don't have to really clean," I said, "I'll clean up first and then you can just do a little dusting."

He stepped past me into the hall then turned to face me. "Swear you're okay?" He held out a piece of paper. "Oh god, don't worry about me," I said, accepting the paper with one hand, clutching the door with the other to hold myself up. "I'm totally, totally fine. Thanks again."

"Okay," he said, "call me, okay?" I glanced down to see a phone number on the scrap of paper. "Definitely," I said. He smiled sweetly. "Don't forget, okay?" He turned and went down the stairs.

The next night the evening condensed itself into a gray ghost dripping like latex inside me from the lattice of my bones and cigarette after cigarette disappeared into its web. The black sky poured in through the window with its flotsam of car alarms, sirens, shattering bottles, trucks shifting gears. I dozed off. A girl dropped by to see me while I floated and I asked her nicely, "Please." The sun turned light blue, gasping in its haze.

 ZIPPER MOUTH

In the painting Jane gave me I see witches growing from a small hill or the top of a newborn planet, these witches are also trees. I see a sky with three wobbly objects like lavender clouds, green shadows sailing across the ground. Over the horizon a small tree or perhaps a yellow cloud on a brown stick, growing up from the curving earth. Incoming signals in origami packets, a translucent-winged insect named Jane sailing in on a paper boat.

Once my so-called boyfriend and I split a quaalude then went out for margaritas at El Coyote in LA, where you could see such luminaries as Exene Cervenka and John Doe from the band X. My first 'lude, I couldn't believe it. I was suddenly transparent, just like the world and its workings, which, I now understood, I had completely misinterpreted. We had two drinks and of course wanted more but I was afraid we'd slip into comas like Karen Ann Quinlan so we left the bar, moving through the neighborhood of silvery white trees, both of us as weightless as the eucalyptus currents circulating among the foliage and lawns. In the warm snowy blur of the quaalude my thoughts drifted to the other episode in my life of such lucidity, when I'd been given a shot of Demerol in the emergency room where I'd been taken for sudden kidney failure. I was fourteen and so scared of needles that I involuntarily knocked the syringe from the nurse's hand. But once the medicine drenched my muscles and spread, I thought of the needle with erotic affection. I bobbed in my bed, gliding on a tropical Demerol lagoon, loving my parents, the way events in my life strung themselves into a perfect equation. Things would be fine. My dad was very sad and also a torture machine, but I would fix that, because now I understood everything. I had the math.

A young doctor interviewed me gently, standing next to the bed, taking notes, checking things off, baffled by the origins of my illness. "Ever done any speed?" he asked. Tentacles of association whipped about and tangled in my mind. Driving fast? Had I "done" fast driving? Relation to kidneys—what? I stared at him in a paroxysm of cognitive dissonance. "Speed?" I said. "Never mind," he said quickly. Weeks later I realized what he was asking and was mortified at my stupidity because of course, duh, *speed*, I was hip to the scene, I watched the news. I was also mildly offended and disappointed; all he could come up with was "speed freak," like it was my own fault, when I'd thought him to be a man of perception, who sensed my fascinating wildness. In my mind I drove recklessly and out of control, thrill-seeking nonstop for that place called the Future, a forest populated by intellectuals like, I mistakenly assumed, the fraudulent doctor, as well as philosophers and painters and whatever, who waited in thickets and groves to engage me in art projects and erotic intrigue, not that I had any idea what that meant.

It was late summer when my kidneys shut down after I'd been collected from two sublimely parent-free months in the mountains, where I'd lived on candy bars in a little red cabin next to a hot springs pool. I was the lifeguard, looked after by fun-loving newlyweds Chad and the dazzling Nanette, with whom I was conducting a torrid affair in my mind, her total excellence and dark curly hair canceling out the buzzkill of her disturbing name. I was so lovesick and traumatized by our separation that I commandeered the TV den to lie on full weeping display for days, sitting up only to grab more Kleenex or move the turntable arm back to the beginning of "Hello It's Me." Nan and I were clinically insane over Todd Rundgren. One night she fixed me my first-ever cocktail, a drop of Bacardi in 7-Up, I think, with grenadine and a cherry, and we swam beneath the stars while "Hello It's Me" blasted repeatedly from Nan's Corvette parked next to the diving board, until the humorless Chad shouted at us from the red cabin to get a grip.

I wanted to die being back home and I almost did. In the ambulance Dad held my hand as I hallucinated all the way to intensive care, strung out on my own toxins as we screamed down the interstate.

A gas is one of four states of matter. If heated high enough it enters a plasma state in which the electrons go so crazy with energy that they leave their parent atoms from within the vapor. Drowsily I watch the sway of the IV bottle above me in the ambulance. I'm wavy, rocking in and out of dreamtime: I have a high fever, getting higher. What distinguishes a vapor from liquids and solids is the vast separation of the individual particles. The fluid slides up and down inside the glass and starts to steam. Dad is in the ambulance. In my veins the medicine boils and I lift off, bubbling up from my body the way underwater spherules stream toward the surface from thermal vents. I rise to float around, twirling in the lazy sky. Dad is unaware of the electromagnetic pull dragging his atoms closer together, the infinitesimal acceleration downward into density, skeins of light growing sticky around us as we drift high above the toy ambulance speeding along on a mercury thread.

A film loop runs through my consciousness with the persistence of tinnitus: *Dad in the Afternoon*. Slack figure, business suit, swollen face sliding down toward loosened tie in his darkened bedroom, silent in overstuffed chair next to the king-size bed, his life force a thin black stream leaking up from his aura into the grinning mouth of a demon hovering at his shoulder.

"Take the typing class," he instructed on the days when he was Good Dad, professional, kind, and in con-

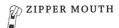 ZIPPER MOUTH

trol. "That way you'll have something to fall back on; everyone needs typists." Okay, Dad, whatever. I learned to type in the tenth grade and I was fast like the wind, possibly because of bonus dexterity provided by eleven years of piano lessons, not that I could manage to practice more than ten seconds a day. But who cared? We lived in a neighborhood of mumbling cadavers who emerged to gather the mail before returning to their solariums and sliding glass doors, walls rippling with sparkle from the pools where their gelatinous anima floated, face down. I'd be poor, pay cheap rent for my garret; I'd be incandescent, thermonuclear with the Joy of Art and Living Free.

I shivered, discharged from the elevator into the fluorescent hallway with its hospital tiles outside the glass walls of the temp office. Inside the agency sweet and chipper boys in white shirts and Dockers with their hair greased into facsimiles of hair plugs scurried about the grey environs. Were my icy hands too stiff to impress these philistines with my awesome velocity at the keyboard? Clipboards were distributed, data obtained, tests administered, fractions flunked by me. I knew the drill, I'd worked for hundreds of agencies, a million jobs. For years, in cities far and wide, I'd worked the machines, starting on the ground floor at age ten with lawn mower and clippers, steadily working my way up with discipline and elbow grease to soda fountains, cash registers, spinach factory conveyor belts, typewriters, phone lines, dictaphones, typesetting apparatus. Salad spinners for caterers during the desperate hours. I had higher degrees, notwithstanding my incomprehension about how to use them to design a career.

I completed the tests and was led to the desk of a tiny child named Sandra, dressed professionally in a beige suit crowned tastefully with a taupe wedge haircut. "I'd like to familiarize you with our philosophy," she said, handing me a brochure from which leapt the sentence, *We strive to achieve Core Values to live by superbly well.* "Did you enjoy the fractions portion of my test?" I asked Sandra, hoping to cheer her up. "Yes, it's really fun here," she agreed enthusiastically, looking really confused.

Dear Sylvia Plath:
Hi I am fourteen and I know you're dead but it's 1 a.m. and my dad is swearing and falling around in the pool like a drunken pork sausage. What a fucking asshole. I was standing in the kitchen two seconds ago with a butcher knife ready to go kill him before he shoots us to death, but I chickened out. I know your dad was a problem too so I could totally relate to your poems about how he's a Nazi who kept you living in his boot even though I basically hated poetry until this minute. So I'm just writing this fake letter because NOW HE'S GETTING OUT OF THE POOL LIKE A MONSTER AND SAYING FUCK. Jesus Christ, Sylvia, if you could hear

him, it's like he's not even human. Now he just massively fell back in. Achtung, you Nazi motherfucker, just drown and get it over with so I can relax. Listen, Sylvia, I can't believe you stuck your head in that oven, you crazy nut! I'm completely terrified to die, even though vastly depressed. There is so little time in this life to do what you want, more on that later.

I had to look out the window because it got all quiet, but he's just slumped over in the grass like an ape. It's sad but fuck him. Anyway, Sylvia, I've been tortured about dying for years, ever since reading *Little Women* made me realize we're all doomed and it ruined my life. But one day, I opened your book *The Bell Jar* and literally died of shock. For the first time I saw someone in a book portraying emotions that were exactly mine. I never even knew it was okay to write about them! I never would have figured it out by myself. Like when you said how the tulips were breathing, I realized I always saw them breathing too but I was in denial. Oh my god I fucking HATE feeling bad for him after he just scared the shit out of me all night. I try not to but I can't handle him being all lonely in the grass like that. He seems so ashamed and confused, like he doesn't know what's happening and no one can help. I don't want him to slip and die for real, just knock himself out a little so I can sleep. Even though then I'll dream he's chasing us with the gun. I always want to tell him don't worry, it's not your fault, everyone loves you, we'll figure out how to make it stop, but I can't. Being insane and not human when he's like this, you can't get him to make sense, plus no way am I going out there alone. He's like a bear who never learned English and seems sweet and nice when you pet him, but all of a sudden you feel a fang in your brain and a massive cracking sound blasts your eyes out, as slowly you realize your head is being crushed to death in his rampaging jaws!

Sylvia, there's so much to express but it's a school night. I will tell you more later. IF I am still alive tomorrow. How perfect would it be if my dad killed me tonight and they found this letter under my body, all smeared with blood.

Dear Sylvia Plath,

Like you, I have been sensitive and depressed all my life. Ever since Beth went out with the tide in *Little Women*, my mind has been a dark chamber full of death. But did or does anyone hear my choking sobs of entrapment? Answer: no. My debate teacher Mr. Walker ("Greg") is this amazing person, age twenty-four. His hands express gently and he really likes your poems. The only other guy I know who does is my friend Russ Marcus; he smokes pot in his car. We hang out in the parking lot every day during Social Studies and even though he's totally nice to me he's still popular. Well, there's this depressed older girl Marla in the other debate class. Greg's always saying in his caring way how sensitive and brilliant she is because she's depressed and writes poems for the literary magazine. I've only read one poem by her, about a spider. I didn't really get it. And even though she's in Debate I barely know her because she's too sensitive to compete. Greg says she's too shy and can't handle very much except reading Emily Dickinson. This is so frustrating because I'm unbelievably shy too on the inside, but he doesn't understand. We talk about your poems but I don't know what to say that's intelligent. I've been trying to show my depression more so he will see I'm smart but basically all I do is joke around with him like one of the guys. He's hilarious plus I get a little hyper from boys shooting me with spitballs during Rebuttal. I wish I looked more tiny and delicate. Why am I always laughing even though worried about being murdered? (By my dad mostly, but basically by anyone.)

Well, I have been giving a lot of thought to this one poem when you go, "Love, love, my season." A man such as Greg has not run across my path before and now that I am in my Season of Love you have helped me a lot. When the Season first started I was overwhelmed by torture. Yet, Sylvia, you made me see how suffering is beautiful, instead of getting down on myself. Fuck Emily Dickinson. Even though I've never read her I'm at least as depressed as Marla. Also, not to be mean, I know how the spider is a metaphoric bug of sadness, etc., but it still seems like poetry is mostly for assholes, no offense, but I'm trying to get past that.

I think Greg will see the pain behind my laughing façade if I can write like you. But not LOOK like you, ha!! I'm sorry, you can't help it that you were in the '50s with those hairstyles. I picture you like

Jacqueline Bisset, except with glasses. Does that sound shallow? I guess that sounds shallow. Don't worry, I don't need to be attracted to you to like your writing. But it would help. Not that I'm a lesbian. I just need these visual aids to get into it or something. What am I talking about, I'm grossing myself out. I don't think anything about anything. You're dead and this fake piece of shit is over.

Dear Ms. Plath:
Please forgive me for troubling you when you have no idea whom I am, and of course you mustn't feel the need to answer as this is doubtlessly one among thousands of letters from your admirers. But anyway, I recently had the pleasure of being introduced to *The Bell Jar*, and to your poems. I found myself quite moved, to my surprise. I never knew there was a poet as superior and perceptive as yourself. I am unfortunate to be trapped in a small farming town in the middle of NOWHERE much like Jane Eyre, where we only get four channels with nothing edifying on them. I deeply adore and write poems thanks to you, which Mrs. Gunn my French teacher says are quite interesting, but please don't think me immodest for I know they suck. I am surrounded by oafs who are nice to me unless I act like I like or love them, for example Mr. Jim Tedeschi but fuck him he's simple country folk, forgive my language. Often I am swept by tantrums, being tempestuous.

To get to the one worthless bookstore, Mother must drive me to the mall on the freeway that stretches like a flat black tongue through hellish corn. The people rise from the dead to drive their glittering cars like shattered cries speeding into the throat of madness. Like you I am masticated in the grinding jaws of endless thoughts of death. One example: I couldn't drink out of a glass when I was seven because I thought glass would come off and slide down my throat, bleeding me to death. If anyone is reading this in the future because they are writing my biography or snooping in my room as usual, looking for fake reasons to punish me, this part of my journal is private and not for publication. I am just thinking out loud because unfortunately I am surrounded by zombies who care nothing for inspiration and passion, just hunting and vacuuming, saying how negative I am every time I say something true like how commercials on TV are total lies and people are sheep. And speaking of lies, this is not being written because I am smoking pot as I am constantly accused of by a person or persons who say they can smell it on my personage when I come home, which is a total paranoid falsehood. It just so happens that my pot smoking is for purely personal reasons, totally unrelated to my diaries or other creativity ventures.

So my point as a straight-A student with many extracurricular activities such as marching band and jazz band is that I smoke pot in my usual responsible way and not as the lazy criminal who feeds off society, nor also for some meaningless high, but rather as a positive thing that increases my productiveness by slowing my brain down

enough to sit still without being carpet bombed
by a herd of worrying about tumors and where is
Dad.

Blood is spurting like a seizure
Do you not hear the tulips
screaming in the vortex?
The carefree child became a monster
No more shall the small bee merrily prance

Or . . .
Carefree child you are a monster
    Or so the zombies say
Whom once was an innocent baby
    Explodes in the screaming vortex
Stabbed by the prancing nightmares
    Of a voodoo doll in a bloody seizure

Is this one better?
See the bloody Voodoo child of seizures
Laugh at her hanging naked
from your inscrutable rope
Do you not hear her stygian screams
Above the malodorous vortex?
    That is filled with the
snapping bones of Madness?

               Snapping madness
               Of Bones?

Madness of Snapping
    bones?

 ZIPPER MOUTH

God, poetry is HARD. Trying to find the perfect way to express the visions trapped inside me is like being a tiny bird pecking against the stone mountain of eternity. How can I be a madly brilliant artist with burning eyes and arms like sticks if I can't even have a nervous breakdown! If someone would think to take me to a psychiatrist like they took Sylvia Plath, the truth of my invisible SOS would be revealed by an expert, proving this hell house. But no. Being so burnt out from planning the vacuuming schedule, the only thing you see is pot. Making up excuses to punish me for no reason whatsoever, it never occurs to you that a girl with massive feelings about this magic life might stay in her bedroom all the time because like all serious artists she is depressed, for example, by all the sadness and death in the world, starting with CERTAIN THINGS IN THIS HOUSE!!

Also I wonder why this person or persons think they know what pot smells like because there is no way certain parties have ever been within walking distance of a joint . . . MOM. Oh right, I'm too stupid to know you obviously hate me because I know all your friends stay drunk so they don't have to face the fact that their lives are meaningless even though they have a pool.

As I write this, Sylvia, my parents hurtle toward death in their sleep, strangled by the scarves of apathy wrapping their noses. I sit on my bed surrounded by the accoutrements of my lost childhood, looking out my window.

The moon is weeping in the window
    of my prison cell

Where I am swinging naked
                    (in a noose)
        above the
            Bones
                of
                Snapping
                    Madness
                            Where
                            is
                            the
                    ghostly lover
who will be my

                    phantom teacher
        Do you not see me   BURN?!

    Your initials are enigmatic
                Your first name rhymes with Egg . . .
        Yes I am haunted!
                Yes! How I yearn
                    for you to get this rope off of my
                                                Neck

    so I can suffocate
                in your lugubrious
        caress

The night Jane told me about her dream of being on the mountain, with Damon down on one side and me on the other, the night I confidently withheld from her the glittering gift of my kiss, a tactical error which haunts me to this day, I walked Jane to her doorstep and said goodbye. She tossed her cigarette, drew out her keys, and kissed me lightly on the cheek, glancing briefly into my eyes. "Well all right," I said. "Okay!" I watched her walk through the filthy yellow atmospherics of the marble hallway. I lingered nonchalantly outside the ornate black bars across the door glass until Jane reached the first landing and turned to smile, firing off a last shot of green before disappearing up the stairs. I headed home past the church with its verdigris brass dome overlooking the tenements. My radiating sexuality blistered certain passersby and zapped others to human-shaped pillars of ash that remained upright for an instant before collapsing into silky heaps on the sidewalk.

The black parachute of night flapped transparently around me as I floated, the avenue in motion, memories of walking at night from the train along corrugated streets to X's apartment when I first moved here, how strange to me, what did I use to worry about, I guess the future, or how to order deli sandwiches without making an ass of myself in front of the natives.

That's when I lost my virginity to the mime!" Jane yelled one night at a party, the first time we met, delivering the punch line to some anecdote as the group standing around her laughed. *Why do I know that's true?* I thought, as a friend steered me toward her to introduce us. I'd been dying to meet her, she was deeply cool, I'd read a review of her latest performance. *When this girl is onstage, linearity flies out the window*, the reviewer wrote, and I had gasped internally. *Why, I too am nonlinear!* I thought. She was hilarious and charismatic. I felt pretty good-looking too. I'd dressed up. I wasn't drinking that night but fortunately someone had weed. I stood spellbound before her, the way she talked was so pleasurably disorienting. Her observations and syntax seemed channeled from another solar system; half the time you couldn't understand a single thing she said. Well, you could, sort of. How well I recall the sidelong glance directed at me when she said, "I was just lying there thinking 'I need love so badly, but instead what I will receive is work,'" as I passed her the joint. An outbreak of alarm flared across my skin at my own predictability, though I affected bemused confidence, a somewhat detached air suggestive, I thought, of a fascinating and seductive interiority. Jane drained her cocktail and took a long drag off the joint before passing it on. "So, anyway," she continued, exhaling, "the demand for clarity is making me have a psychotic break."

Driveway, basketball in my palm. Sunlight glances into my stomach, a punch of beauty from cement, black poles of the carport, bricks of the red chimney I slam the ball against. Summer before seventh grade, "Spirit in the Sky" blasts from KFXD on my radio hooked to the extension cord. Music is a green wave coming into me, love will feel like this when it enters, when I meet you, you will do this to me coming in. I hold my straw like a cigarette, cock my hip, and lob the ball with one hand.

When the Rossmans are out of town I push the mower along the sidewalk toward their yard in a yellow bathing-suit top and electric blue bellbottoms that at long last fit snugly at my hip bones. I remember these pants and my body in them, everything suddenly perfect, my legs in the stunning blue cloth that dropped into a sexy flare, my arms feeling good in the sun. I felt sad that this was the last summer I would be a twelve-year-old girl. I watched from outside myself as I walked down the quiet summer street past the houses; I saw this body disappear, pulled forward into other versions, shedding itself behind me.

I stumbled from the airport that morning hungover and stunned by the late August weather which seemed the breath of evil itself. Suffocating in the sun's white metallic glare, I was dressed in sweatshirt, jeans, and boots, which might as well have been a snowsuit. I passed out on the bus from the airport and a guy had to wake me at the station. "Miss!" he shouted. "Miss!" I stood on the street reeling, panicked at the masses hurtling past, realizing in horror that I'd left my sunglasses on the bus. I arrived in my apartment to find outgoing calls on my phone cut off for mysterious reasons, probably involving money. Back on the street, I made an anxious call to Gia, who wasn't home. Wasting crucial beer quarters in my search for a working pay phone, I felt insubstantial yet spotlit, an apparition exposed to the sting of rapid-fire humiliations as I moved naked, peppered with smirks and accusing glances, through the bristling crowds.

Upstairs I drifted off to sleep, while Steve and Cherry nosed about me in welcome. Someone called to ask about my vacation, to which I replied, "It was fine, I had a religious experience with a moose but now I'm going to kill myself." Last night at the airport I was so smashed I almost talked a woman out of her Valium before wandering into a lounge where, in order to exoticize my loathsome identity for the drunken businessmen whom I proposed to charm into buying me drinks, I adopted a French accent that oscillated randomly through an eclectic hybrid of Middle Eastern, French, and Nordic. "I do not barely speaking zee Inglis!" I slurred, swaying. "What is going on here for you crazy nuts tonight!" Later, on the plane, I wandered up and down the aisle until finally a guy gave me a Sudafed just to make me go away.

My alarm went off. I looked at the clock. How could it be noon? In happiness, at 2 a.m., I'd breathed in. Now, at noon, in horror, I breathed out. I was supposed to be at work. "Oh my god," I moaned. I'd managed to snag a job of sorts and I couldn't fuck it up. After months of unemployment, lying on my bed, borrowing from friends, I'd allowed my life to fall into a state in which I was rarely required to show up for anything at all. I felt panicked, I was double, was many, vibrating on the bed, feeling my body accelerate backward without me. There I was, traveling moodily anorexic in an old car through Death Valley—this really happened—my somber lover, who loathed me, driving as we listened morosely to lush discordant punk, both of us feeling alienated in the French cinema style, the car's interior erotic with the heat of our narcissism. We were in our early twenties and our grandiosity came to nothing. Simultaneously I sit at my desk pretending to study biology in junior high, worried that I'll laugh so hard I'll wet my pants, dogged always by the heavy questions of existence. I walk home from kindergarten, run from a stranger, swallow a quarter accidentally which was intended for my popcorn at the drive-in, view my dad in a coffin, hear the term "night sweats" for the first time. My desires and options are autumn leaves, their leisurely spiral erratic with updrafts and dips, teasing feints and side swirls. How tantalizing is each leaf! Yet how impossible to attend its performance all the way to the ground! Other leaves twirl into the picture, flirtatious and distracting so I lose track of the first.

Of course I had days of optimism, when a random, unfounded sense of happiness possessed me, and on such days I ventured forth from my bed and into the city, filled with a fervor to perform tasks, initiate productive new business relationships, renew social bonds, etc., but invariably these high spirits mingled with sadness at my many inadequacies to form a lethal fuel that propelled me into all sorts of inebriated adventures, the recovery from which took sometimes days, sometimes weeks, until I felt first better, then great, then fantastic and glamorous and thrilled by the brilliance and talents of my loving circle of friends, a cycle during which my longing for a grip, for the hearty glow of a person who pays her rent on time, accelerated like the revving engine of a car stuck in mud, the whine in my brain climbing higher and higher while I filled my date book, threw cash around like a sultan, and strode flirtatiously through the streets. The happier I felt the faster I had to walk, then run, my brain a cotton candy machine, fear the pink sugar, spun until it filled my skull. Oh my fucking god. I couldn't possibly go to work, I couldn't possibly not go to work. I was even out of nickels and dimes for the change-sorting machine, my trusty friend at the A&P, the awesome Coinstar 3000.

Once Tony decided to try methadone, so he scored a cupful from a junkie exiting a clinic and drank the whole thing. Only later did we learn that a common trick of meth-clinic regulars is to pour the drug into their mouth under the watchful eye of the nurse and pretend to swallow, then spit it back into the cup when they get outside and sell it. Anyway, Tony drank his new elixir as soon as he rounded the corner. By the time he got home, he was virtually paralyzed and couldn't see. His vision was blurred for days. Since he'd already called in sick to his new job every day that week, he needed a hardcore excuse. It was a twenty-four-hour agency and the overnight receptionist didn't know Tony's voice. So he dialed and said he was calling for Tony, who'd flown back home, an emergency, his little niece had drowned. I called him at work the next day and was informed in hushed tones of his niece's death. When I left a message of condolence and concern on his machine, Tony called back almost immediately and said, "No one's dead. You've got to get over here, I can't see. I just found out I took about five times as much methadone as you can handle if you're not strung out on dope." Which he wasn't, not yet anyway.

"Everything goes so slowly when you're waiting for a check to clear or trying to get a giant rat out of your kitchen, but then all of a sudden you're sixty-five," Jane remarked as we sat in a booth drinking Manhattans with cherries skewered on tiny pink plastic swords. "I feel like I'm stuck in a tar pit attached to a rocket going faster than the speed of light."

"Something spooky's going on around here," I said. "I'm trying to drink this cocktail slowly but I actually finished it before it got here!"

"I know." Jane nodded. "I dreamed all my teeth fell out. It went on for hours and I couldn't wake up but when I did I'd only been asleep for ten seconds."

"In my dream I'm standing at the counter," I said, "where I have spent the entire day trying to get a goddamn spear of broccoli ready to steam and then I wake up and it wasn't a dream."

"Why are vegetables so hard?" wondered Jane. "Mmm," I replied. We ruminated thoughtfully, sucking on our teensy pink swords while the music blasted.

"Yeah, vegetables," I sighed heavily. "But don't let me pull you into the screaming vortex of my lesbian mental illness." A drag queen with a microphone started to sing along with the music.

"Well, your vortex is more interesting than mine," Jane shouted over the pounding beat. The people next to us looked over. "Well it is!" she informed them loudly.

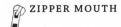 ZIPPER MOUTH

"What is?" I shouted back. "What is what?

"Your fucking vortex. More interesting." The air started to hum slightly between us. Sipping her drink, Jane lifted the corners of her mouth around the straw and raised an eyebrow. The mirror ball spun and colored galaxies flowed across her face. O enchanted microsecond when an utterance unveils a glimpse into the dark recesses of the beloved, when a sparkling curtain rises on the tiny stage starring Yourself in spectral illumination, an image around which constellate the mysterious feelings of the one you desire, a girl named Jane, facing you, as inaccessible as you are to yourself, two live girls separated by table, cocktails, skin, whispering fictions, the body itself is 99 percent empty space, subatomic particles winking in and out of existence. Just say anything, Jane, open your mouth, make me gasp. We breathe in, I laugh, we breathe out, you laugh. Glasses melt into the table, this is science, everything is sentient, the table grows transparent as we pass through it easily into each other and there it is.

I drove through the West Texas desert, which seemed entirely composed of ground-up bone. The vacant landscape was chalk and the carburetors were making that weird noise. I was twenty-five, I was drunk, my first car had burned to the ground when I'd put the clamp wrong on a gas line and it sprang a leak onto the molten head of the engine. Bam. I'd had it for three months. Three action-packed months during which I broke up with my boyfriend, left LA to return to college, and my dad sailed off a cliff in his Jeep. They didn't find him for days, his head submerged in its own fluids near the gas pedal, more pools of blood on the backseat floor, our two labradors pacing anxiously hundreds of yards above on the asphalt.

I thought the desert was the coolest thing, very barren. At that point in my life I felt myself to be a genius though photos later revealed me to be somewhat swollen. Hangover wracked my nervous system as I drove, and I prayed for a gas station to come along so I could get a Corona for my nerves. When a little Texas Chainsaw Massacre-type store came into view I bought a six-pack and soon was careening down the empty highway high as a kite, reflecting on the relevance of the Joy Division song blasting from my boom box, certain that sadness had evaporated from my body to create the supernatural light in the landscape around me. It came through the window, a strange light washing across my hands on the wheel; in my throat, a decay of filmy language and a cigarette between my lips. The blue sky beyond my windshield leaked pigment along its edges, gushed blue across the hood while withdrawing as I drove till my body was just a craving, straining to swallow something that wasn't there, like trying to lick the colors in a movie.

I got out of my car to piss and tinker with the carburetors. The car was another ancient Volvo, same as my first one; it made me feel cool and rebellious. My boyfriend had shown me how to fix it. I wore a blue velvet dress. Alcoholically I considered, *If Rimbaud were born in a toxic waste dump would he wear a blue velvet dress.* I was so drunk I dropped my screwdriver into the depths of the engine. The car was parked on a shoulder that plunged hundreds of feet to a bleak and treeless body of water, a secret cistern, probably, of contaminants, since at one end of its sterile banks was a cluster of military-looking Quonset huts, metal tonsures aching in the sun. I pissed burning into a red vapor circling my legs, heat waves flowing up persimmon in the afternoon glow. I was caught in a magnetic field, my defects resolved into focus—there's your weird hair, your voice, your smile. Grayness opened its mouth to swallow me down. I rummaged in the glove compartment for a map. Whew.

Brain surgery had been the life plan, inspired in grade school by the Time Life books. Oh sure, when I brought the cow's brain home from the meatpacking plant to dissect for my seventh grade "science project," not that I had formulated such a project or even knew what dissection entailed—I imagined that once applied, the scalpel would take over, revealing colorful sections of the brain labeled Eyesight (chartreuse!), Love (pink and orange!), Memory (ultramarine!), Other (psychedelic!)—I took one look at the gelatinous mass, threw up, begged Mom to get it away from me, and abandoned my medical career. Another dream dies, flash-frozen in an instant of searing ontological shock like those woolly mammoths revealed by melting glaciers, encased forever in an ice age that struck so suddenly their tongues were layered with flower petals, unchewed.

Outside my window it was cold, bare trees shaved in a bitter wind. Or maybe it was summer, who can know. The TV's dismal flow leaked across my sheets. Jesus, close eyes. What did the day used to be like. I drifted to a memory of a happy time when I brought home a poem in second grade about clouds. "Clouds" was misspelled: *The fluffy clods are floating in the sky.* My mother's loving laughter, my beautiful young mother, at the time she would've been thirty-one, her laugh a fizzy feeling, both of us dissolving into giggles, sadly ignorant of the bloody five-car pileup of life I was hurtling blissfully toward.

Memory neurons adrift like soap bubbles leaked threads of melody from records my parents had danced to late at night in the living room when I was five. Down the hall, framed by my bedroom door, they swayed in leisurely embrace, shuffling through the dim glow to things like "Satin Doll," which now formed the soundtrack to other diaphanous shots of a rosebush behind the house across the street where these two older kids named Shawn and Mark had buried their brother Wayne beneath the back porch, unconscious but still alive, after a gun accident. Even though the brothers lived next door to my best friends Kip and Kristy, who played with everyone, we never played with Shawn and Mark, they were just wrong. Their house seemed like it came from a dark world on TV. Supposedly Shawn and Mark were cleaning a shotgun when it discharged accidentally into Wayne's jaw. They thought it was empty, of course, but even I knew to keep a gun pointed down at all times even if you were positive it was empty, even if you'd checked it a million times. After the body was discovered we rode our Stingrays up and down the alley past Shawn's backyard, where, disappointingly, the porch was concealed behind a huge piece of plywood spray-painted KEEP OUT THIS MEANS YOU!

As a seven-year-old grammarian I noted disapprovingly the lack of a period, or even comma, after KEEP OUT. Small crimson roses crept along the margins of the sign and their smell mixed in my head with the sweetish odor of decomposing flesh that had aroused neighborhood suspicions in the first place. A few days before the cops showed up, Shawn mysteriously appeared in my yard and impressed me deeply by climbing up my pine tree, really high. Everyone always said he was weird and I guess he was; he didn't meet your eye or talk much, but actually he seemed pretty nice. Where had his mother been, I wondered later. I glimpsed her sitting on their front porch once or twice, a shapeless fat thing in a pinkish-gray nightgown blinking at the street like a toad. I had been a tiny body on a Stingray. I found my house keys and checked to make sure no cigarettes were burning, avoiding the mirror above my kitchen sink.

Dreamy dream: we are leaving. Pack up all the people in my head, load them in the car. We're going outside now, take a little ride. My head melted into air and I leaned against a building. A coppery heat trickled from the sky and you could taste it. I often felt that I was about to drain upward into the flammable ether, leaving my body to crumple on the concrete below. Swept up now in the flows of jabbing, vindictive pedestrians, I remembered the dream and felt my molecules pull apart into vast distances. My head melted, or maybe my skull, releasing the particles of my being in a great rush. Out they fled into the scorched air, quantum multitudes streaming up from their lockdown in the crushing predictability of my flesh. Surprised at this sudden weightlessness, the particles of my being balanced delightedly on the light around me, a host of number-less organisms, homunculi bobbing up and down on the heat's glassy swells. "Smile, honey," someone yelled. "It might never happen." I looked around but he was lost in the boiling crowd of pedestrians—dripping foreheads, surging ahead, enraptured by vengeance.

I was a vessel for nightmares, and I moved through the world as a hologram, my body transparent inside its outlines, its surface flaring with savagery snagged from passing airwaves. Boneless secretaries crawled across me, a hitchhiker slithers up the driveway, undulating over the crease in my shirt. A station wagon dips into the fold of my eyelid, glides up my brow, slows down to cruise a few Children of the Corn bouncing red balls in unison at my hairline. I'd dash into *Today's Candy* for a liter of *Good-O* orange soda, conscious of the wee doctor flitting up my spine. Joke with the perv at the cash register, thinking *What an asshole*, even as a pyramid of bikini girls water-skied into my ear. These beings chattered without pause but I couldn't hear them, their sagging lips opened and closed over runny teeth, conversing with invisible others in a lost tongue. I knew the language they spoke was long dead and I felt so lonely. Orbiting my rib cage a girl with an earache holds out her hand for some pills. Mom and daughter rippling in and out of focus at my throat chakra, they're sitting on some basement steps, mother holding tiny pink roller skates wrapped in a satin bow, kissing daughter's head. In the girl's hands a cupcake with four lit candles, girl gazing bedazzled up at mother's face. Mother spectacular, sparkling in a shimmery corona aglow on a background of fireworks and pinwheeling stars. There was no hope of translation because these creatures confided and promised according to an alternate physics in which I didn't exist and couldn't. At night the broadcasts began when I tried to sleep, fragmentary dramas erupting on my skin. A dad and four kids, say, prowling a field, their guns passing in sinuous waves through the wrinkle of my jeans near the zipper. Nurse with picnic basket slinking along my ankle toward a playground, feral children spiraling up my leg, their ghostly knees and hands skimming my hip bone before they slid off to vanish in the sheets.

Sometimes the mirror was still dizzy with you. I pulled myself from the brick wall and made myself walk home, at first stepping gingerly, testing each leg for signs of collapse before allowing it to take my full weight, while at the same time trying to disguise my difficulties from the hostile throng, which required strenuous concentration, because it was necessary to tiptoe during the interval before concluding that my foot could be planted solidly and with conviction on the ground. I adopted an air of nonchalance, feigning interest in the city's architecture, though actually

I couldn't see it, I was practically blind, all my senses were focused on whichever leg was in the process of touching down, my entire consciousness located in the supporting thigh. Then, once I had judged the possibility of a buckling knee to be minimal, there was the issue of pushing off and swinging the back leg forward. Plus I had to avoid knocking someone down. There was also the problem of the sidewalk itself. I was pretty sure it might suddenly swing down in front and up behind me to ninety degrees, a seesaw, no longer the ground but a vertical wall or chute. My stomach flipped as I walked and my internal gyroscope plunged from side to side. Is this machine going to slam me into the pavement and when it does, will it take a long time? Will I feel everything as it happens, second by second, feeling like years, going around and around, faster and faster, speeding up until I'm flung, as though from a slingshot, into the sky above the fairway, where I remain while my body drops away, loose change drifting down from my pockets giggling. The sun she is gorgeous but the golden tresses of her rays fall tumbling into the abyss and are lost.

ACKNOWLEDGMENTS

This slender volume took a village of family and friends, elite medical professionals, CIA remote viewers, spiritual advisors, and Navy Seals to keep me on track as the book itself spun wildly out of control. To name the people who deserve my gratitude could easily triple the length of this book, but there are some without whom it simply wouldn't exist. In this regard Elizabeth Reddin, with bewildering enthusiasm, scrutinized the manuscript countless times; her wisdom kept me on point when my eyes were twirling in my head and her passion kept me going. Eileen Myles has from start to finish not only offered me her brilliant literary acumen but rocked my world with her love and unflagging support. Cecilia Dougherty and Nicole Eisenman applied their vigorous critical visions at various stages, lasering open new portals of insight as though with a Tesla death ray. I am deeply indebted to Karen Braziller, who from sheer generosity read the manuscript closely not once but twice and offered critical guidance that helped me move forward.

ZIPPER MOUTH

For the grants and residencies that provided me with time and head space to work, thank you to the New York Foundation for the Arts; the Fine Arts Workshop in Provincetown, MA; the Millay Colony; and most especially Edward Albee and the Albee Foundation on Montauk, Long Island, where the book first began to take shape.

My agent Rosanna Bruno took me on as her last client, championed the book, and negotiated me through many a hair-raising pitfall; I am truly grateful for her support. Thank you to Don Weise, for his faith in the book and getting the project off the ground. And I am beyond thankful to my publisher Amy Scholder for bringing the book to the finish line with verve, patience, and liberating insight.

For their supernova hearts and the incalculable effects of their artistic fire, generosity, inspiration, and comedy stylings on the DNA of my work, I am forever indebted to Charlie Atlas, Bob Blome, Lizzy Bonaventura, Paula Cronan, Kyle de Camp, Angie "The Douche" DuFresne, Rosemary Hammer, Tony Harold, Harrison, Faye Hirsch, Katurah Hutcheson, Annie Iobst, Mike Iveson, Angela Lyras, Carole Maso, Rachel Moore, Tom Murrin, Joe Reiner, Lori E. Seid, Lucy Sexton, Julianna Snapper, A.L. Steiner, Tony Stinkmetal, Michael Taussig, Michelle Tea, and Joe "Westy" Westmoreland. And hey, Le Tigre, thanks for the shout-out!

Thanks above all to my wondrous and insanely energetic mother for loving me infinitely with trust and patience while at the same time fighting to save the birds and other wildlife of Idaho.

Finally, Nicola Tyson heroically stepped in during the final stages of the book's composition to reinvigorate my process and help me sort through disparate ideas. I am forever grateful for her commitment and zeal.

ZIPPER MOUTH

The Feminist Press is an independent nonprofit literary publisher that promotes freedom of expression and social justice. We publish exciting writing by women and men who share an activist spirit and a belief in choice and equality. Founded in 1970, we began by rescuing "lost" works by writers such as Zora Neale Hurston and Charlotte Perkins Gilman, and established our publishing program with books by American writers of diverse racial and class backgrounds. Since then we have also been bringing works from around the world to North American readers. We seek out innovative, often surprising books that tell a different story.

See our complete list of books at **feministpress.org**, and join the Friends of FP to receive all our books at a great discount.

THE FEMINIST PRESS
AT THE CITY UNIVERSITY OF NEW YORK
FEMINISTPRESS.ORG